SPARROW AND THE STREAM

A HUMAN-MADE LO-FI TECHNOTHRILLER
WRITTEN BY A REAL PERSON NAMED

F.C. SHULTZ

Daath Stone Books

FIRST PRINT EDITION

ISBN: 979-8-9930307-2-2

Cover Design: F.C. Shultz

Typesetting and Formatting: F.C. Shultz

to families who forgive.

CONTENTS

ONE

Sparrow knew the odds.

Her mother had been missing for two weeks. Sparrow cried herself to sleep every night for the first ten days. Now, she just sobbed at random moments in the day while she went about her chores in The Castle, the abandoned fire watch tower where she lived with her mom.

Or, used to live at least.

Her mother taught her how to survive in the barren woodlands of western Tennessee. Sparrow knew how to search for food in the abandoned houses on the hills of suburban Hornbeak Village. Her mother taught her to go down to the southwest and scour the farmland for tools. She knew to keep the gate to The Castle locked to keep the bears out. She could fish Reelfoot Lake for dinner whenever she needed. She knew Zero City existed to the north, and that she was to never go there.

She knew she was never to cross The Great River that flowed down from the mountains and created a border around the only land she'd ever known. She knew she was to never cross The Concrete River either, that flowed east to west. And she was never to fly over the mountains that hugged the eastern edge of the forest where The Castle was tucked.

She knew all this, the odds, and the dangers, but still she asked.

"Hobbes, what are the odds mom will return today?"

Her bedroom was a small, square room in the upper level of the fire watch tower. A single bed, a pole with few clothes hanging, and a telescope filled the space with ease. Sparrow felt the thin, frosty air seep through the cracks of the tower as she took the four steps to her makeshift closet. She pulled on her favorite outfit: insulated long underwear, the color of tree bark, her mother's faded, light red, button-down shirt (she rolled up the sleeves to her wrists and the bottom of the shirt fell well below her backside), a dark, moss green vest, and an old pair of tan, brown hiking boots with creases throughout. Then she pulled on her favorite item of all, her vintage leather football helmet.

Her mother brought it back from one of her supply runs and Sparrow fell in love with it. It wasn't so bulky and heavy that it made her neck hurt and limited her mobility, like the motorcycle helmet her mother used to make her wear. The leather had softened with age, and it covered the scar above her left ear perfectly.

Hobbes calculated the odds almost instantly, but being a robot designed with social awareness, it tried to deliver the news delicately.

"Miss Sparrow, there is a one in nine thousand four

hundred and thirty-three chance your mother will return today."

The spherical, metal ball floated above the hole in the floor which led to the main level. Its three propellers rotated in unison, carbon fiber blades slicing the air in near silence, as Hobbes moved fluidly throughout the room. It was such a small machine that Sparrow could hold it with both hands when its propellers were folded inside its metal shell.

"That's much worse than yesterday," Sparrow said.

"That is correct," Hobbes replied.

"Why? It's only been fourteen days."

"It's April second and the temperature dropped below freezing last night."

"Mom is smart. She probably just made a fire to stay warm."

The windows were boarded so light could not enter. Sparrow went to the north-facing window and slid the wooden panel to the right. The window was frost covered, but the sun was already shining through, melting the ice.

"That is a real possibility. Dr. Hoodia has keen fire-making skills," Hobbes replied.

"She's still out there, Hobbes." Sparrow pointed the telescope out the window and began surveying the land, looking for any signs of life. "She has to be."

"Of course, Miss Sparrow."

"Skies are clear," Sparrow said with her eye on the pale blue sky above Reelfoot Lake a mile north. "When was the last time we took the motor out for a search and rescue mission?"

"March twenty-seventh."

"March twenty-seventh," Sparrow yelled, pulling her face away from the telescope. "We've got to go today. The weather's looking better, and it's been too long."

"I must remind you that we have done nine missions by foot since then. You've been a very vigilant daughter." Hobbes flew just out of Sparrow's reach and just above her head. The smooth voice sounded nearly human, save the lack of vocal inflections on certain words.

Words like daughter. He had pronounced it "dot-er."

"It's not enough," Sparrow said as she pulled the panel back over the window.

Hobbes turned on a flashlight built into its shell. "We'll take the motor and fly north to expand our radio signal."

Sparrow went to the hole in the floor and climbed down the ladder in the opening. Hobbes followed her.

She reached the main floor of the watch tower. Windows filled the walls of the tower. Each window was covered by a wood panel. Her mother designed the wood panels to slide on tracks, so they could stack behind each other during the day, covering just one window. She began sliding open the panels above the sink and countertop. A water tank was strapped above the counter with a hose leading to the sink. Next to the counter was her mother's desk.

She continued sliding the panels around to an empty wall until she got to the corner, diagonal from the kitchen sink, where the door going out to the walkway was located. She pushed the two panels around to the south wall where a cushioned recliner sat next to the solar panel battery hub. A small coffee table and couch filled the middle of the room opposite of the recliner and battery.

Finally, she let the panels rest in the last corner of the room, where her mother's bed was nestled. The sun had burst over the hills and filled the room. Only the corner with her mother's bed, covered with the wood panels, lay dark.

"According to the historical records, we are due for severe electrical storm activity in mid-April," Hobbes said.

"Are you fully charged, Hobbes?" Sparrow pulled an egg and a small pan from under the counter.

"Ninety-three percent."

"Better get on your dock. Might be a long day."

"Of course, Miss Sparrow." Hobbes moved through the air and landed inside a small bowl on a circular table like a hummingbird trying to find a feeder.

"And anyway, how old is that data?"

"You know I am a closed network robot. Dr. Hoodia designed me to function independent of The Stream with the purpose of helping humans through knowledge—"

"And undeniable facts. I know, Hobbes." Sparrow cracked an egg on the corner of the hot pan and dumped it into the heat. "That's old info. You have facts up until what year, again?"

"September ninth, two thousand fifty-two."

"Hobbes," Sparrow said with an excited urgency, "I was only four then. You don't think things change in eleven years. They do! Everything changes. Stuff changes.

I know the world didn't used to be like this. I've read the books. Things change, Hobbes."

The egg was smoking in the pan. Sparrow wiped a few tears from her eyes. "Why don't you power down for a while. Charge faster. I'll power you back on when it's time to go."

"Of course, Miss Sparrow." The hum from Hobbes' internal processor shut off and the tower fell silent.

The sizzling of a burning egg echoed off the walls. The burnt aroma filled Sparrow's nostrils. She let out a little scream and lifted the pan off the hot plate and set it on a bright blue oven mitt that read Yellowstar National Park System in faded white cursive script.

She took the plate and the oven mitt to her mother's desk and sat down. She stared out the window while her breakfast cooled. The morning sunlight painted the tops of the evergreens a lighter shade than their shadowed bodies. They stretched as far as she could see. The mountains to her right were the only things standing above her tower. Despite being so early in the spring, a few geese flew overhead near the tower.

Sparrow grabbed the two-way radio from its charging stand. The antenna had been duct-taped back on after she dropped it from the paramotor last year, but it still seemed to function fine. She took a deep breath before turning the radio to channel four and began speaking.

"Bird's nest to Albatross. Do you copy?" She released the thick black button on the side of the device.

Static.

"Bird's nest to Albatross. Do you copy?"

The static shorted and the sound of scratching came through the speaker.

"Mom, is that you?"

The scratching ended and was replaced with the familiar static.

"Closer. I have to get closer." She rose from the desk. "Hobbes." The circular red light on Hobbes' sphere shell turned green. Three propeller blades unfolded and spun in one action. Hobbes floated above the circular table housing the charging station.

"I'm listening, Miss Sparrow."

"We're taking the motor out today."

"I must remind you we have approximately four hours of energy left in the motor."

"Four hours! That's plenty. I can't sit up here and wait any longer. We've got to look farther."

"Of course, Miss Sparrow."

Sparrow pushed the chair under her mother's desk and grabbed the radio. She clipped it onto a loop on her vest before climbing the ladder up to her room. Before Hobbes was able to map out the room and follow her to the second floor, she was climbing back down with a dark green rucksack over her shoulder, a solid oak bo staff taller than her with grimy white tape around the center, and tinted snowboarding goggles resting on her leather helmet.

"Is that everything, Miss Sparrow?"

"That's everything," she said, looking across the landscape like a captain at sea. "Let's go flying."

Sparrow opened the door to the fire tower and felt the frigid air attack her cheeks. She let Hobbes fly through and shut the door in a vain effort to retain the heat trapped inside. She leaned over the rail and looked down the seventy feet to the ground below.

"Hey, Hobbes," she said, still leaning over the ledge. Her feet were coming off the wood plank floor. "What are the odds I'd survive if I jumped from here."

"Oh, Miss Sparrow. I would not advise an action like that."

"What're the odds, though?" She looked over and gave Hobbes a devilish grin. "One in a hundred?"

"I could only hope they would be that good." Hobbes had now flown over the railing and was facing her head on, trying to ease her back onto the deck surrounding the tower. "That would be like falling into the ice on Reelfoot Lake."

"One in five hundred?"

"Oh, dear. Those are the odds of surviving a bear attack." Hobbes was now bumping against Sparrow's helmet, trying to push her back to safety.

"Tell me the odds and I'll get down."

"You are an ornery one, aren't you?" Hobbes flew back over the deck and floated silently for a moment. "One in five thousand forty-nine. Does that satisfy you?"

"Sure does. Thanks, Hobby. Now, on to the motor, yes?"

With this, Sparrow followed the deck around the perimeter of the castle. The roof overhung far enough to block any rain from reaching someone standing out on the deck. The boards creaked under her steel-toed boots as she ran by. Finally, she turned the second corner and approached the tall metal cabinet filling the space where the deck ended. It was the size of two refrigerators, side by side, with a chain around the handle. She grabbed the lock and put her fingers on the four spinning combination dials.

"Okay, I can do this. Remember, Sparrow. Remember." She closed her eyes and focused on the four numbers she needed to recall to open the lock. She spun the first dial under her thumb. "Just need the first one, then the rest will come." She opened one eye and squinted at the rusty silver spinner. "Zero-Nine-Zero-Nine."

She turned the dials to match her epiphany and the lock popped open. A bright red nylon blanket hung overflowing from a bag on the left side. She stuffed the abundance into the bag and slung it over her back.

"You must complete the pre-flight checklist before ascending." Hobbes' voice echoed off the metal interior of the storage unit. "Dr. Hoodia's rules, you know this."

"This isn't my first hot rocket, Hobbes. I'm going to do it," she said, as she unhooked the large metal fan from the back wall. "I always do it." She pulled the motor and propeller clear of the storage unit and set it down. She slammed the doors shut and swiped the dials before grabbing the machine and starting the process more boring than the pre-flight checklist.

Carrying the motor down seventy stairs.

The propeller was housed in a circular metal frame, which allowed Sparrow to carry it with her hands at ten and four. She bent her knees and lifted the rig two inches off the ground. She guessed it weighed about forty pounds, but she had no real way of knowing.

"Watch your step as you descend," Hobbes cautioned her as she rounded the corner. The robot ball was hovering in front of her. "I don't know what's more dangerous, propelling yourself through the air or trying to carry something bigger than you down all these stairs."

"Have I ever fallen down these stairs?" Sparrow said, eyeing the first step.

"You have not," Hobbes replied.

"Exactly. Why don't you meet me at the gate?"

"Of course, Miss Sparrow." With that, Hobbes throttled his propellers and flew over the ledge. Sparrow heard the buzzing of its propellers grow faint. The forest silence returned. Wind pushed tree branches together mimicking a waterfall. The tower swayed in the wind, ever so slightly, causing the wooden floorboards to creak. That was her cue to get to the ground.

She was able to peer through the blades and the metal frame cage, but the solar powered motor blocked her view of the first step. She closed her eyes, took a deep breath, and thought, "I've done this a hundred times."

She threw her weight forward and her foot landed on the first step.

Her eyes popped open, and she brought her other foot forward and began her descent.

The tower was in relatively good shape for being well over a hundred years old. The wooden cross beams were supported with rusted metal beams, forming large X's up the side of the tower. Countless steps had been repaired or replaced. The frayed, braided, metal handrail was seldom used to avoid getting poked by the metal fibers. Sparrow's confidence grew with every step.

She reached the second to last level and a chain link fence sprouted up around her. This was the only adjustment her mother had added. "To keep the curious animals away," her mother had reasoned. Sparrow had to set the motor down on the ground to unlock the gate and slide the door open. She pulled the motor through and slid the gate shut, locking it back in its place.

"Glad to see you made it in one piece," Hobbes greeted her as she was picking up the motor.

"Find a good takeoff spot for me?" Sparrow asked.

"I believe Lincoln's Trail will do. The path is clear of debris with a slight negative elevation."

"I'll do the checklist over there." Sparrow took off in a sprint toward the trail. Hobbes tilted its propellers toward her to keep up. The motor was getting heavy, and all Sparrow wanted to do was get in the air. Her run slowed to a speed walk as she struggled to keep the metal casing from hitting the ground.

She came to a clearing in the trees where the path went downhill to the south. She put the motor down and looked back toward the tower. The trees hid the stairs she had just conquered, but the top of their castle was visible.

"Maybe I could boost the radio signal," Sparrow said, still eyeing the tower. "We could head back up to the tower and use the metal from the lamp to extend the antenna."

"I believe that could add a minimal extension to the range." Hobbes circled her and flew in front of her at eye level. "Is that what you would like to do?"

She looked at the little cabin suspended in the air for

a few more seconds before shaking her head. "No. I've stayed up there too long. Besides, this is just a little recon flight to extend our range. It could even be..." Sparrow hesitated, "fun."

"Are we ready to begin?"

"Chute is first, right?" Sparrow asked.

"Correct. Unfold the parachute and spread it out evenly along the ground, with the straps facing the direction of takeoff."

Sparrow slung the bag off her back and unzipped the opening. A mess of red parachute exploded out of the bag.

"So, I'm a bad folder. Big deal," Sparrow said, prompted only by her own conscious. Finding one end of the red fabric, she did her best to separate the parachute and lay it flat on the grass. It took nearly ten minutes to get it laid out properly.

"Easy enough. Hook the chute to the motor next, right?" Sparrow asked.

"The next step is to check parachute integrity," Hobbes replied.

"Ugh. That step is so boring." Sparrow walked a circle around the open parachute. After her cursory inspection, she declared, "No holes. Looks great. I'm hooking it to the motor now." Four black carabiners the size of her open hand lay at the end of the parachute straps. She grabbed them one by one and connected them to the back side of the propeller, where the seat was.

"Check motor battery percentage," Hobbes said,

anticipating the next question. Sparrow pushed a small red button on the top of the box behind the seat.

"Sixty-seven percent," Sparrow yelled back. "Forgot to plug it back in last time. Should be plenty if we stay at a low enough elevation, right? Won't put too much strain on the motor?"

"That is correct. Elevations of seven thousand feet decrease motor efficiency."

"We just need to get close to Zero City, and then come back. Seven miles straight shot if we go over the lake?"

"That approximation is correct," Hobbes replied.

"Help keep us at the right height, okay, Hobby?"

"Of course, Miss Sparrow."

"Let's stop talking about it then," Sparrow said louder than anything she'd said previously. She bent down and found the pull and yanked as hard as she could to start the motor.

Nothing happened.

She remembered her mother showing her how to pull the cord in a steady motion by keeping her strength even. She tried again. Focusing her strength, she felt the resistance on the other end of the cord and pulled the motor to a growling start.

She lifted the humming motor onto her back, with the propellers rotating, ready to push her forward. She buckled the straps over her shoulders and across her lap. With both hands, she pulled the snowboarding goggles over her eyes, and the forest became a bit darker.

"Come on, Hobbes," she yelled above the purr of the motor. Hobbes lowered into her open hands. The three propellers collapsed into the sphere, and a carabiner took the place of one of the propellers. She clipped her friend onto one of the remaining loops of her vest. Then, she found the four cords that led to the parachute and lifted them above her head, like she was about to do a pull up with them. Air filled the chute and Sparrow felt the resistance. She leaned forward and started sprinting.

Faster and faster, she ran down the path. The cords in her hands began straightening out and she knew the parachute was raising up. She continued to run half the length of a football field, downhill, before it happened.

Her feet left the ground

TWO

The ground fell away and the blades of grass became a green blur. Thick evergreens shot up in her line of flight. The clearing was coming to an end as the path curved back through the woods. Sparrow had each hand through a loop of rope tethered to the parachute. As she pulled, air filled the red fabric and lifted her higher into the air.

The loop cradled her wrist as she held the blade speed button. She pressed it, and the blades came to life. A moment later her toes brushed the tops of the trees as she ascended.

She pulled with her left arm and circled around toward the watch tower. She rose higher until she was even with the top of the tower, then held her elevation, throttling the motor to the lowest gear.

"The Castle looks strong as ever. See anything that needs fixing?" Sparrow yelled over the low hum of the motor and propeller blades.

"Structural integrity approved," Hobbes replied.

"Away we go," Sparrow said. She pulled both loops as close to her body as possible, increased the blade speed, and shot even higher. The watch tower looked like it belonged with a child's set of action figures from her new height. The landscape opened, revealing miles and miles of forest to the south, and the ghosts of skyscrapers to the north.

She pointed herself toward Reelfoot Lake and let off the throttle a bit. The engine relaxed to a purr and the blades moved with ease. She let the wind from the south push her forward. The trees were waves of green, dark and light, rolling with the hills where they were planted. The mountains alone stood taller than her, daring her to cross over to see what lie on the other side.

"Think mom will let me cross the mountains when she gets back?" Sparrow asked Hobbes.

"There are no good things beyond the mountains. None at all. Everything you need is within the bounds of the mountains and great rivers."

"Sometimes I just want to see what's beyond, though. You know? What else is out there? Don't you get frustrated knowing your information is limited to everything before eleven years ago?"

"I have the entirety of recorded history available for download from The Stream. I do not remorse over those lost eleven years. That would be like a farmer mourning over one bad apple while standing in a one-hundred-acre orchard. Preposterous."

"But you can never gain any other information. Mom won't let you connect to The Stream. You can't know what's going on in the world."

"You should not be caring about The Stream. Dr. Hoodia would not approve."

"Dr. Hoodia should have come back to The Castle, then," Sparrow said. Tears ran down her cheeks, filling the bottom of her large goggles.

They flew in silence. A few birds passed by and looked at the paramotor floating on the breeze. Reelfoot Lake grew larger like a loaf of bread rising in the oven.

Sparrow pulled her arms down, tightening the rope, causing them to gain elevation. Cold air became nearly unbreathable as they touched the clouds. The motor growled with the strain.

"We're at eleven thousand four hundred and sixty-two feet, Miss Sparrow."

"Higher up. Longer range. Better signal," Sparrow said with empty breath. She looked around at the splotches of green forest beneath them, surrounding the puddle of the lake. She had lost visuals on their watch tower during the ascent, but now she could see the roads to the east and the dark snake, that was The Great River, far away in the distance. The buildings of Zero City were more numerous in the northern horizon.

Sparrow clipped a short rope to the radio with a carabiner and removed it from her vest. She turned the knob, and the red power light came on. Green station number lights indicated channel four. But, before she had a chance to get a word out, an elderly, scratchy voice filled the airwaves.

"Anyone good out there? Battery dying. Me too. Need to get west. In the rail—" The voice was gone in a snap. Sparrow checked her radio to see if it had malfunctioned, but the light still shone red and the numbers green.

"Did you hear that?" Sparrow asked Hobbes.

"I think we better focus on finding Dr. Hoodia and stay out of trouble," Hobbes replied.

"He needs help, though."

"Perhaps you could try another station," Hobbes said. Sparrow found a new frequency. Static filled the space around the paramotor suspended in the air. Twenty seconds later, a child's voice filled the station with an eerie cadence, like the words were being read from a script, not spoken from desperation.

"Umm. Hello? Daddy says—I mean, please meet us —me, in the big park. We—I need help. Big dogs attacked. Hello?"

Sparrow turned the radio off.

"A trap?" Sparrow said.

"Indeed. Those not in The Stream tend to be the more aggressive type, statistically speaking. Which is why they were flagged and banned."

"That first man didn't send goosebumps down my spine, though," Sparrow replied. "It was different."

"Of course, Miss Sparrow."

"I need to keep checking the stations. Mom could be trying to reach me from a different frequency."

Sparrow switched the motor completely off, bringing the overall volume level down. The only sound was the wind swirling circles around them. She turned the radio back on, found a new station, and set the radio in her lap. Then, she adjusted their position, letting the wind fill the parachute so they maintained their altitude and position over the lake.

She did this sequence multiple times over the next hour as she checked for any sign of her mother.

Most of the stations were white noise static. The voice of the eerie little girl filled numerous stations, but she never heard the old man from the rail-something again. The white noise stopped when she made it to channel six. She held the radio tight on her ear.

"Nimda!" a young man's voice yelled through the radio. Sparrow dropped the radio and held her ear in pain. The radio fell off her lap, dangling ten thousand feet in the air, only connected by the metal hook.

With one ear ringing, she found the radio and held it within earshot of her other ear. The voice continued. "Don't be joyriding, Nimda. Bring that tank back. He'll pop your eyes if he finds out you're wasting his find."

"Tell Mydoom to go to hell," a second voice replied, though it was hard to distinguish the differences. "Good luck trying to call again, Sasser." White noise filled the frequency again. Sparrow waited for a response from the first man, who she assumed to be the one called Sasser.

"Flaggers, no doubt," Hobbes said after two minutes of white noise.

"That must mean we're in range of Zero City," Sparrow said, excited with the revelation. "We have to keep searching the stations."

"I might suggest we lose some elevation, Miss Sparrow. The wind makes it quite difficult to hear anything at this altitude."

"Yes, right. Good idea."

Sparrow clicked the radio back onto her vest and grabbed hold of the parachute cords. She raised her hands to dump some of the air from the parachute to bring them closer to the ground. The cold air stayed in the higher elevation, and the air above the lake was still. Sparrow unclipped the radio from her vest and turned it back on.

"Bird's nest to Albatross. Do you copy?" she said into the microphone. "Bird's nest to Albatross. Do you copy?" She released the button and waited for a response.

Static.

White noise.

She turned the radio up one station and tried again.

Same result.

Sparrow hovered over the lake, flipping through the stations, saying the passphrase for nearly an hour. She would have gone longer, but the radio battery died. There were a few responses, but most of them sounded dangerous, and none of them were her mother. She dropped her head.

"Where is she, Hobbes?"

"I wish I knew the answer to that," Hobbes replied. "As you know, her tracking device lost signal nine days ago."

"What is the last location we have for her?"

"Hornbeak Village."

"Northwest, right?" Sparrow asked.

"That is correct, why do you—"

The motor roared to life with the press of the button in Sparrow's hand and they were jolted from their holding pattern. The flaps of her helmet fluttered in the headwind. She pulled down with her left arm and they banked hard to the left, toward the east. Gravity pulled Hobbes out of Sparrow's lap toward the lake, but the carabiner held. The hard-left turn had made them parallel with the ground. She pulled with her right hand to even them out.

The water was right under them now. Sparrow remembered her mother telling her not to get too close to the water when flying, because a still pond reflects the sky like a mirror and it's hard to tell where the water starts. Depth perception is all screwy above a still lake. But she couldn't resist.

Remembering her mother's warning, she dropped slowly toward the surface. Then she pointed her toe and drug it along the surface of the water.

It rippled a peaceful wave in opposite directions. They were approaching the edge of the lake, with trees surrounding. She pulled down with both arms and they lifted into the air, just above the trees.

A two-lane highway bordered the lake and Sparrow followed it north for a few minutes. It split off to the west under a faded green sign that read "Hornbeak Village 3 miles." The main highway continued north under a metal sign, spray-painted black, with the words "Zero City - Turn Around," painted in white.

Sparrow turned to the left and followed the westbound road.

She slowed the motor down so she could scan the landscape for any movement.

The road rose and fell with the hills. Sparrow could not see much of anything in the cover of the woods, so she kept her focus on the road and the occasional clearings. There was nothing to be found.

She reached Hornbeak Village in no time and crisscrossed the winding roads of the neighborhood. Brick houses with tattered roofs peppered the area. The yards were all overgrown and most windows had been broken from Flaggers or other vagabonds.

Hobbes showed her exactly where the last signal was received from the tracker, but it was the middle of a soccer field.

"She's not here," Sparrow said. "I know we checked this spot already, but I don't know what else to do."

"I'm sorry, Miss Sparrow," Hobbes replied. "I'm estimating we have twenty-two percent power left in the motor."

"We can go home." Sparrow gave the parachute cords an unconvincing pull and they rose slowly. "I just thought there'd be something. Some sign of her."

"Shall we try again, tomorrow?"

"I don't know," Sparrow replied.

She followed the rolling road back toward the highway. She pulled her ski goggles from her face and let them rest high on her forehead. Her head fell back, and her eyes faced the sky. Sadness and the wind in her face made her eyes water.

A few moments later, a gust of wind came from nowhere and nearly blew the goggles off her head. Out of pure instinct, she leaned her head forward and clasped the goggles by the strap before they flew off. Doing this, she was forced to look toward the ground. Her tear-filled eyes caught a glimpse at something moving. She wiped her eyes clear to get a better look and couldn't believe what she saw.

Three people walking toward Hornbeak Village. A man, a woman, and a younger girl.

She knew none of them were her mother, which sent a shiver down her spine. The young girl waved her arms to get Sparrow's attention. But Sparrow was not interested.

Sparrow faced the southeast, grabbed the throttle and turned the motor to full power. She flew over the trees, abandoning the road, and made a beeline for the watch tower. She arrived in record time, ran up the flights of steps, shoved the paramotor into the storage bin, and ran inside, locking the door behind her.

She pulled the wood panels closed around the room to block out the light, before turning on the generator and heading up the ladder to her room. She turned on a lamp, pulled off her vest and threw it on the ground. Then she jumped into bed and covered herself in a heavy down blanket, where she stayed the rest of the day and night.

"Hobbes, will you stay up here with me?"

"Of course, Miss Sparrow," Hobbes replied, landing gently on the floor next to her bed.

The night was restless.

Sparrow tossed and turned and awoke with every howl of the wind and call of an animal. At one point, the fence around the entrance to the castle shook like a metal rattlesnake. The sound echoed up the tower.

"It's them," Sparrow said. "It's those people. They've come to get me."

"I'm sure it's just some curious wildlife," Hobbes replied. "Happens quite often, though you usually sleep through it."

The chain-link clanging continued.

"Will you go check? I'll open the door and you can go fly down there and check."

"Of course, Miss Sparrow."

With Hobbes in agreement, Sparrow crept out of bed with the down blanket covering her head to toe. She climbed down the ladder and made her way to the door. Hobbes hovered behind her.

"Tap on the glass three times when you want me to open the door," Sparrow whispered. She unlocked the two deadbolts and cracked the door open a foot. Hobbes flew through with ease. She closed the door behind him, re-engaging the deadbolts.

Then, she waited.

THREE

With her back to the door, she slid onto the ground. The darkness of the room caused her to doze off seconds after Hobbes left, but her heart had not forgotten the potential threat just outside and continued to beat wildly. This pattern of wake, sleep, wake, sleep went through three or four cycles before the knock came.

Then, two more.

Sparrow scrambled to her feet, unlocked the door, and opened it slowly. Hobbes was flying at eye level. She opened the door further and her robot companion flew in.

"Was it those people?" Sparrow asked.

"No, it was a—"

"Grizzly bear?"

"No, Sparrow. It was only a—"

"Mountain lion. They can jump high, you know. And climb. We've got to build the fence higher when Mom gets back."

"It was a raccoon. It found a large walnut inside the fence and reached through to grab it, only to realize its hand would not fit back through the hole in the fence while holding the walnut."

"A raccoon?"

"That's right," Hobbes added. "I flew down there and flashed my light a few times, and it ran back into the woods."

"Okay. A raccoon. Alright," Sparrow was saying to herself. "Thank you, Hobbes."

"Of course, Miss Sparrow. Back to bed?"

"Yes, right." Sparrow walked back over to the ladder. As she was climbing, she caught a glimpse of her mother's empty bed in the glow of Hobbes power light. She closed her eyes as she continued her ascent. Seconds later, she collapsed into her bed. She heard Hobbes click into its charging station.

"Hobbes, are you coming?"

"Of course, Miss Sparrow."

Hobbes flew up through the hole in the floor near the ladder and landed on the floor next to Sparrow.

"Good night, Hobbes."

"Good night, Miss Sparrow."

THE NEXT MORNING Sparrow felt like a new person. Her confidence grew as she slid the wooden curtains away and the sunlight filled the tower. She turned on the hot plate, pulled out the skillet, and started cracking an egg in it. Then, she sat down at the desk with her two-way radio and began the process of trying to communicate with her mother.

An hour passed and Sparrow heard nothing but static on all the channels.

"It's not working, Hobbes."

"Perhaps we can try again later." Hobbes replied from its charging station.

"Okay." Sparrow put the radio back on the charger.

"We skipped your agility training yesterday," Hobbes continued. "Dr. Hoodia would not like to hear that. Up for some sparring?"

"Yes. Okay," Sparrow replied. "I'll meet you down there." She stood from her chair and opened the door to a cold, April draft. Hobbes flew out and she closed the door behind him before climbing up the ladder to her room. She pulled her vest off the wall and secured her leather helmet to her head. Once she was dressed, she walked over to her bed and got down on one knee, so she could reach underneath. She searched around blindly before finding what she was looking for.

Her bo staff.

The wood was cold and solid in her hand. She felt ready to go outside now that she held her protection. After giving it a few whacks into the open air, she put it over her shoulder and slid it into its leather-looped sheath on the back of her vest. With her new energy, she bolted down the ladder, across the room and out the door.

She locked the deadbolt with the key on a string around her neck (the other deadbolt could only be locked from the inside) and started her climb down the steps. She could see Hobbes as a dot of blue on the green grass below, and it reminded her of how small the people had looked yesterday. She had never seen people on the ground from her paramotor before. Her mother had only let her fly solo in the last six months. They usually flew tandem.

She reached the bottom and unlocked the chain-link gate. Hobbes sat in a sunny spot with a one foot by one foot square of solar panels coming out of the sphere and facing the sky. Sparrow approached the robot.

"What is your battery level?"

"Forty-eight percent," Hobbes replied.

"Forty-eight? Okay, we'll get you plugged in after training."

"Yes, Miss Sparrow," Hobbes said. The solar panel separated into three pieces that folded in on themselves, until they were small enough to fit back into Hobbes' pale blue metal shell. The panels were replaced by three propellers and Hobbes took flight with a low buzz.

"Which protocol would you like to run today?" Hobbes asked.

"Which one does Mom use?" Sparrow asked.

"De Oppresso Liber."

"I don't know what that means, but let's do it."

"Very well."

The propeller blades whirled to a higher gear, causing Hobbes to move in a zig-zag pattern with newfound speed. Sparrow pulled the bo staff from her back and gripped the tape, holding it at even center. She fixed her eyes on Hobbes, flying around like a wild banshee, and waited.

She studied the pattern of its flight. Noticed a consistency. Then took a swing.

Miss.

"You'll have to be much faster," Hobbes said. "Much faster...little bird," it repeated, but this time playing a sound clip from some old T.V. broadcast with an ominous male voice. Sparrow did not like that.

She strung together three, then four, jabs and swipes with the bo staff. Hobbes dodged them all and kept its distance as she continued to step forward. The deep male voice laughed. Then it morphed and distorted into a high-pitched, teenage-girl squeal before speaking again.

"Knew she couldn't do it. What a momma's girl. Wah wah."

Sparrow let out a scream.

She over-emphasized a forward strike with the top of her bo staff, which caused Hobbes to dodge left. She anticipated this evasive maneuver and shifted her momentum to attack with the bottom of the staff in quick one-two succession.

It worked.

The bottom of her staff struck the underside of Hobbes' metal shell. Hobbes immediately retracted all the propellers inside of its body and fell out of the air. The faux enemy hit the ground with a muted thud.

"Hobbes!" Sparrow yelled. She sprinted over to her fallen friend and picked it up. A small indentation was present where Sparrow had made contact. "You alright?"

The light on Hobbes' shell flickered back on and the propellers came out of their openings, lifting Hobbes back into the air next to Sparrow.

"Well done, Miss Sparrow," Hobbes said in its normal voice. "I must say, the odds of you completing the De Oppresso Liber were terribly low."

"I thought I killed you," Sparrow said.

"It'll take more than an old wooden stick to get rid of me," Hobbes replied. "Shall we continue your training?"

"What's next?"

"Cardio."

Sparrow groaned.

"Try to keep up," Hobbes said, before zipping off down a westward trail through the woods. Sparrow sheathed her bo staff and followed behind. The canopy of trees overhead cast deep shadows on the trail. Bugs chirped and creaked as she ran by. The smell of pine filled her nostrils as she gasped for breath. Hobbes turned on its flashlight so Sparrow would not get lost. She sprinted full speed to catch up.

Once she reached her guide, she was able to keep up by jogging at a comfortable pace.

"What if we run into those people?" Sparrow asked between breaths.

"I've got my thermal sensors scanning the area. That won't happen," Hobbes replied.

"Oh, okay," Sparrow said. "What are the odds they know something about Mom, though? Maybe they've seen her?"

"Very low," Hobbes replied. "The odds are one in twelve thousand six hundred and four."

"Hmm," Sparrow said. They ran on a bit longer, Hobbes leading them through different trails, cutting through the forest around the tower. They came to a small creek and Sparrow asked if they could take a break. Hobbes approved.

"Where are we?" Sparrow asked. She found a large tree and sat at its base.

"Two point one miles northeast of the tower, Miss Sparrow."

"So, the lake is up there?" she said, pointing to what she figured was north.

"Correct," Hobbes replied.

"The highway is probably close, then, too."

"What are you getting at, Miss Sparrow?"

"I'm sorry, Hobbes. If those people know something about mom, I have to ask them, even if it puts me in danger."

"Miss Sparrow, I'm afraid I cannot allow—"

"Fly back to the castle, then. Wait for me on the deck," she said. "Though I'd much rather have you with me."

Lifting off the rock it rested on, Hobbes flew suspended in the air for a moment. "Very well. Only to keep an eye on you. I will alert you now if my thermal sensors pick up anything."

"Thank you, Hobbes." Sparrow got to her feet and stared at the sky. The sun was nearly overhead shining directly down on her. She pulled her bo staff from her back and pointed it across the creek. "Is that west?" she asked.

"That is correct."

"We'll head north then, going around the lake,

staying off the highway until we get to the exit for Hornbeak Village. Ready?"

Hobbes did not reply, but Sparrow heard the propellers spin faster, so she walked north along the creek. They had to leave the path to follow the water. This was no problem for Hobbes, ducking and dodging between felled tree branches and overgrown brush. Sparrow, on the other hand, used her bo staff to clear a path.

It was of little use.

Though most of the forest had regrown the leaves lost the previous fall, the fallen leaves and branches still covered the ground below. They were moving too slow, she decided, so she rolled up her pant legs and walked into the creek.

"I think these boots are waterproof," Sparrow said, feet fully submerged in water. A cold pang shot up her leg. "Nope, they're not," she said seconds later, with a laugh. "Too late now. It's starting to warm up though, right?"

She walked with increased speed now that she did not have to clear brush and brambles. The only difficulty was not slipping on wet rocks, but her bo staff doubled as a useful walking stick.

It did not take long for the creek to widen and the water to rise to Sparrow's knee. She could see the creek flowing into the lake up ahead, so she found a spot on the bank to exit, boots squishing and sloshing on the dirt bank. The dust turned to mud around her shoes. She kept walking, until she came across something deeply concerning.

"Hobbes, I found something." Sparrow pointed to the ground with her bo staff, but kept her head on a swivel, surveying their surroundings. Hobbes flew closer to the ground. "What does that belong to?" she asked.

"Scanning," Hobbes replied. "Looks like a female grizzly bear. Roughly three hundred eleven pounds."

"It's an old track, though, right? Like, been there for months?"

Hobbes flew closer until it was hovering three or four inches from the paw-shaped depression in the earth. "Would you like my best estimation?"

"Yeah?"

"Twenty-seven hours."

"Okay. Okay." Sparrow shifted her weight onto her bo staff. "Keep calm. What would Mom do?" she said to herself. She closed her eyes tight and tried to focus, despite regretting coming this far without rations or weapons or her mom. "Check the area for thermal signatures again. Go up higher if you need to get more range."

"Of course, Miss Sparrow."

Hobbes took off, going from a few inches off the ground to above the tree line in ten seconds. Sparrow took a few deep breaths and readied her bo staff in a defensive position. She rotated in a circle, slowly, until Hobbes returned.

"Well?" she asked.

"I have good news and I have bad news."

"Okay."

"The good news is there are no bears in the

immediate vicinity. No wildlife at all, save a few ground squirrels."

"What's the bad news, then?" Sparrow asked.

"Those people from yesterday are making their way toward us.

FOUR

"We've got to hide," Sparrow replied. "I wanted to sneak up on them. Not the other way around."

"I'm afraid they already spotted me," Hobbes said.

"Come on," Sparrow said, as she ran deeper into the forest. She hid behind a tree with a thick base. Hobbes flew behind, following her. With her eyes closed and her back to the tree, Sparrow gripped her bo staff with both hands. She heard bushes and tree branches being pushed aside.

And voices.

"That little flying thing is around here somewhere. I just saw it," a male voice said.

"It's a Class-3 CompBot, Dad. They were super common back when The Stream was just taking off," the voice of a child replied.

Sparrow peeked around the tree and saw the girl, who must have been around twelve or thirteen.

"We're going the wrong direction," a firm female

voice declared. "We're going the opposite direction, actually. Zero City is to the north."

"We're just seeing if that flying person can help us, Mom," the girl said. "Or needs help."

The family had walked past Sparrow's hiding spot, and out of audible range. She could see them making their way south, so she decided to follow behind. As she got closer, she saw they all walked with their arms folded and their hands beneath their armpits. The father, Sparrow assumed, wore khaki shorts and a thin, long sleeve shirt. The mother wore gray dress pants and dress jacket. The daughter wore an oversized dark green sweatshirt that reached her knees, with tights underneath, and a black backpack secured to her back.

Sparrow realized they were walking strangely because they were cold. "Why were they not wearing more clothes?" she wondered.

"We need to make a fire or something," the father said. "It's getting dark and I'm absolutely freezing. Rox, how much food do we have left?"

"Umm...," the girl swung the backpack off one shoulder. "Like ten."

"That's all?" the mother snapped. "We need to get to Zero City. We're running out of time."

"Of course, Teka," the father replied. "First thing in the morning, we'll set a course."

"Let's make a fire here," the mother said, ignoring her husband and pointing to a clearing in the trees.

Sparrow watched as the mother and daughter sat on the ground. The daughter stuck her arms and legs inside the sweatshirt, while the father gathered pieces of wood and stacked them in the clearing. He grabbed something small from the backpack, a lighter, Sparrow assumed, since he knelt to the pile of sticks and held the small rectangle object near them.

Nothing happened.

It was much darker in the woods since the sun had passed over the mountains in the west. Sparrow guessed there was still nearly forty-five minutes of daylight left, but the darkness came quicker this close to the range. The sun being blocked also meant the temperature dropped significantly. The mother was now trying to light the large logs, while the father and daughter sat shivering nearby. Smoke rose from the branches, but nothing more.

Down on her knees in some tall grass to observe the family, she whispered to Hobbes, "I should help them."

"I do not think that to be a good idea, Miss Sparrow," Hobbes replied at a low level.

"Mom always said she used to be a helper, back before everyone plugged in." Sparrow took her bo staff, still in her hand but flat on the ground, and put it back into its sheath on her back. "Scared or not, I can help these people."

She rose to her feet and began walking toward the family.

Despite the failing light, Sparrow was able to get a better look, and could now see the tears in their clothes and scrapes on the father's exposed legs. His beard was thick, but his hair was wispy. The mother's suit jacket had few stains or blemishes, and her hair was wound into a tight bun on the top of her head. The only sign of the outdoors was her muddy boots. The daughter's knees were bulging from the inside of the sweatshirt, and she wore a knit cap with a little red ball on the top. They still had not noticed Sparrow, standing less than ten feet from them, so she decided to speak up as to not scare them.

"Need help with that?"

The daughter, still holding her knees to her chest, fell onto her side. The father let out a short, high-pitched scream. The mother dropped the lighter.

"With the fire. I can help you get it started if you'd like," Sparrow said.

Not waiting for an answer, she walked over to the brambles and picked up the lighter. Hobbes was still flying beside her, keeping out of arms reach of the strangers. Sparrow rearranged the pile of sticks and twigs, placing the smaller twigs at the bottom and the larger sticks on the outside. Then, she walked around the site collecting dead leaves to put under the twigs.

"How does that look, Hobbes? I think that's the right order."

"The odds are favorable. With some added oxygen it should catch."

"Perfect," she replied. She took the lighter and clicked the flame on, placing it against the dry leaves. They caught immediately. Sparrow lit leaves in different places around the fire. Then, she knelt and blew a few short breaths onto the leaves, causing them to glow a bright orange. A few minutes later, the leaves lit the twigs, which enflamed the sticks, and then caught the larger logs. The small fire light danced on their faces as the family rushed in to feel the warmth.

"I'm Sparrow, by the way."

The mother looked up from the flames. Her face was pale, and her eyes were as big as the moon. The father continued to reach his hands toward the flames. The daughter looked up. "Sparrow. That's a cool name. I'm Rox," she said smiling. "Well, technically Roxana Zosia Passer, but everyone in The Stream just calls me Rox."

"You've been in The Stream?" Sparrow asked.

"Of course. Haven't you?"

"Rox, that's enough," the mother said. "I'm Teka, and this is my husband Palo. We're making our way to Zero City for supplies. Do you know the way?"

"Of course," Sparrow replied. "It's dangerous there, though." Sparrow sat down opposite of them, with the fire between, her mind reeling. "What's The Stream like? Where are you from? Why did you leave The Stream?" she asked.

The mother laughed a delicate laugh.

"A lot of questions, huh?" Teka said. "How about one at a time, back and forth? We ask you, then you ask us."

"Okay," Sparrow said.

"I don't like this," Hobbes spoke for the first time.

"Hobbes, power down for a while. Save some battery," Sparrow insisted.

"Of course, Miss Sparrow," Hobbes replied. The spherical robot flew down into Sparrow's open hand, slowed the propellers to a stop, retracted them inside the shell, then powered down. Sparrow clipped Hobbes to the loop on her vest.

"Quite the toy you've got there," Palo said, taking his

hands from under his arms. "What kind of tricks can it do?"

"Is that your first question?" Sparrow asked with a grin.

Rox chuckled a bit. Teka gave her husband a piercing look.

"No, it's not," Teka said before her husband had a chance to reply. "Why don't you go first, Sparrow?" she said. "Start with any question you'd like."

She thought for a moment. The fire crackled in front of them, as embers rose into the sky and disappeared. The sun was gone now, and darkness set in around the firelight. She felt her stomach growl, but tried to ignore it, as a question came to mind.

"Where did everyone go?" Sparrow said. "Like, why are all of the houses and the city abandoned?"

Sparrow caught the family off-guard.

"You don't know?" Rox asked. "Can I tell her, Mom?"

"Sure, dear," Teka said, without taking her eyes off Sparrow.

"Okay, so right after I was born, like thirteen years ago or something—I'll be fourteen next month— there was a breakthrough in virtual reality technology, led by the company FerVR, where Mom used to work. Everyone called it the VR-evolution, because it was the first fully immersive, virtual reality world ever created, and it was affordable. You could stay plugged in as long as you liked, because of how you were hooked in. You didn't have to leave to eat or, you know, go to the bathroom, because there were special tubes that plugged into your arms and stuff."

Rox paused and pulled up her sweater sleeve to reveal a large hole, the shape of a triangle, in her right forearm. It had started to heal but was still a deep red where the blood had clotted. "Then, like eighteen months later, everyone had gone into The Stream and never left, so the cities were just abandoned." Rox paused again. "How do you not know this?"

Before Sparrow could respond, Teka spoke up.

"Don't answer that, Sparrow. We don't want to use our first question like that, do we Roxana?"

"No, ma'am," Rox said, pulling her sleeves back down over her arms.

"I'll go first," Teka continued. "This might sound a bit strange, but do you know how to fix solar panels?"

Palo and Rox looked up from the fire with confusion on their faces. Rox spoke first. "What? That's the question you asked? It shorted out. Who cares?"

"I care, Roxana. Let Sparrow talk."

Sparrow was just as shocked at this question as Rox was. She expected her to ask where she lived or why she was not connected to The Stream. She half expected Teka to ask her the best way to get to Zero City. But solar panels?

"Well, I don't know much about solar panels. Hobbes could probably look and see what's wrong."

"We know what's wrong," Palo said, still looking at the fire. "It got struck by lightning and fried."

"I really don't know much about them. My mom always fixed ours."

"Your mom?" Teka said. She left the phrase open, hoping Sparrow would take the bait.

"Yeah, she's like really techy-smart. Our whole place runs on solar panels. Hobbes too." Sparrow's voice trailed off. The fire crackled as a cold breeze blew through. "She actually went to go find a string inverter or something to repair our panels, but she hasn't come back yet."

"That's sad," Rox said. "I want to ask how long she's been gone, but it's not our turn."

"It's been two weeks." Sparrow took her leather helmet from her head. Shoulder length braids crisscrossed down the sides of her head in loose connection. She wiped her nose with her sleeve. "She's still out here somewhere, though. I'm going to find her."

"That's what you were doing flying around yesterday," Teka said.

"Is that your second question?" Sparrow said, with an ornery smile trying to surface.

Teka, sensing the levity, replied, "It was a statement of fact."

Sparrow returned the smile. "That's right," she said, "I think it's my turn again."

"Of course," Teka replied. She opened her palms to the fire.

"Who are the Flaggers?" Sparrow asked. "Mom talked about them sometimes, but she never told me where they came from. Like, why aren't they in The Stream, too?"

"Rox, want to take this one, too?" Teka said.

"Oh, yes!" Rox replied. She pulled her knees our

from inside her sweater and started moving her hands around. “Okay, so the Flaggers were in The Stream. Like I said, everyone was in The Stream.” She paused for a second, as she looked at the first person she had ever seen in the physical world, who was not her mother or father. “Well, almost everyone. There are rules and laws in The Stream, of course,” Rox continued, “and you have to follow them or else you get flagged.”

“I don’t understand.”

“Flagged is like getting in trouble. Getting checked or reported. Does that make sense?”

“Okay, sure,” Sparrow said.

“If you break the rules, you get flagged. If you get flagged too many times, they kick you off The Stream. They block your tank from connecting, or, if you’re in a facility, they unplug you and escort you out, and then close the doors. It’s terrible.”

“They don’t sound too dangerous,” Sparrow said, feigning confidence. “What’s the worst thing they could do in a virtual reality world?”

The three family members looked at each other.

Teka spoke up. “You already asked your question, dear,” she said, smiling a gentle, comforting smile. “And besides, I don’t think you really want to know the answer to that question.”

Sparrow did not respond, but thought to herself, “If the Flaggers did unspeakable things in the virtual world, what terrible things were they capable of in the physical?” Sparrow needed to find her mother. She was going to get to the point with her next question. But she had to wait. The eager father helped her out.

"Listen, Sparrow. It's obvious you know your way around this physical world better than we do. And we'd really like to get plugged back into The Stream. We just need to go to Zero City and find a generator, or something, that will let us get back into The Stream long enough to request someone to come and fix our panels." He paused, working out the precise phrasing of his question. "So, my question is, if you escort us to Zero City and back to our house, we'll help you find your mother while we're waiting for help to arrive. What do you think?"

Sparrow thought about this for a few minutes while she picked the dried mud from her boots. It was obvious they had not seen her mother or else they would have used that as a bargaining chip. But Sparrow wanted to go to Zero City anyway, so traveling in the big group felt safer, even if these people had hardly any experience in the real world. She had to try something else. The daily radio calls from the tower and the paramotor flights just outside of the city were not working. She looked up from her boots and gave her answer.

"Okay. I'll take you," she said to the relief of the family. "But, if you help me find my mother sooner, she could probably fix your solar panel much faster than having someone sent out here."

"Of course, of course. We'll keep an eye out along the way." Palo said. "Tell us, what does she look like?"

Sparrow's face lit up to the question. "She's short like me, but a little taller. And she's bald."

"Bald?" Rox asked.

"Like a bowling ball," Sparrow chuckled.

"Bowling ball?" Rox said, trying to follow.

"You don't know bowling? You set up a bunch of pins, basically logs, and roll a ball and try to knock them over."

"Why?" Rox asked.

"For fun, of course. They don't have bowling in The Stream?"

"I don't think so," Rox said. Then she motioned to her parents, "Do they?"

"I'm sure they do," Teka replied.

"Maybe on the wacky recreation of history server," Palo said, laughing at his own joke. He was the only one.

"Anything else we should know about her?" Teka asked. "Is she in good health?"

"Yeah, I think so," Sparrow replied. "She's always doing something she calls you-ga and won't ever let me eat any of the candy bars I find in Hornbeak Village, even though they haven't expired yet."

"Yoga," Rox said.

"Huh?"

"It's pronounced yo-ga. It's to help connect the mind and body," Rox explained.

"How do you know what yo-ga is, but not bowling?" She chuckled as she emphasized the new word.

But, before Rox could respond, Teka tried to re-focus the conversation. "Looks like she trained you with the staff, too," she said, pointing to the bo staff on Sparrow's back. "Unless it's just to intimidate your enemies."

"I can use it," she said, a bit offended at the accusation. She stood and pulled the bo staff from her back and held it in a ready position. Then, without warning, she launched into a series of crisp, organized attacks.

Right side, low strike.

Left side, high strike.

Middle jab.

She repeated these various combinations for nearly thirty seconds before ending with a jab, combined with a yell. She held the jab and made sure to make eye contact with each member of the family before breaking her pose and putting the bo staff back into its sheath. She sat back down, cross-legged, breathing heavy.

Rox began to clap.

"That was amazing," Rox said, above her own clapping. "You have to teach me that."

"I stand corrected," Teka said. "I'm sure your mother can hold her own if she has skills like yours with the staff."

"Oh, she's much better than me. I can never beat her when we're training. She doesn't use a staff though."

"No?" Teka asked.

"Nope, she uses her walking stick. Never goes anywhere without it. It's a little taller than mine, but it's more natural looking, like a tree branch with knots and stuff. And it's thicker around the top, where the emerald rock is on it."

"Emerald rock?" Palo asked.

"Yep, really dark green and dirty," Sparrow said. "She got it from..." she paused and thought about it. Nothing came to mind. "Actually, I don't know where it came from. She's always had it."

"It sounds like a sword or something a king would have," Rox added. "Pretty cool."

"Yeah, I guess so," Sparrow replied. "So, yeah. She's got to be fine, because nothing could get that..." she looked at Rox, "sword from her hands. Oh, and she wears these very big, black rimmed glasses."

"Short, bald woman with big glasses and a king's sword," Palo said to himself, loud enough for everyone to hear. "Can't be too hard to find."

"What's her name?" Rox asked.

Before Sparrow could respond, Teka spoke up. "Now, dear, we don't need to get into Sparrow's personal business. I'm sure we'll recognize her mother if we see her."

"It's okay," Sparrow said. "It's Trudy. Trudy Hoodia." Sparrow tried to read their faces to see if the name caused any reaction from the family, but the fire was dying, and the light with it. Teka had turned to get something out of her bag.

"I think she's a doctor, but I don't know of what. Hobbes just always calls her Dr. Hoodia."

"Oh, yeah," Rox exclaimed. "I was going to use my next question to ask about your Class-3 CompBot. It's so cool. What do you use it for?"

"Oh, Hobbes? It does all kinds of stuff. Flies around. Tells me facts and information and stuff. All the information that was on The Stream up to eleven years ago is in this little sphere." Sparrow unclipped Hobbes from her vest and tapped the metal shell a few times. "Hey, Hobbes, wake up."

The light turned on and three propellers extended

from the sphere. They began spinning and seconds later Hobbes was in the air.

"Yes, Miss Sparrow?" Hobbes said.

"These people want to know what you do."

"You're not connected to The Stream?" Rox asked Hobbes. "I've never heard of a piece of technology not connected to The Stream. What's the point?"

"The point, Miss Roxana, is to provide assistance to Dr. Hoodia and Miss Sparrow through historical and mathematical solutions."

"I don't get it," Rox said.

"I think that's probably enough questions for tonight," Teka interjected. "We've got a long day tomorrow."

"I don't mind," Sparrow said. "Hobbes helps me with my training routine, let's me know when the weather could get bad based on historical data, provides data to solve problems based on probability and odds, can scan and identify almost anything in the physical world." She paused for dramatic effect when she realized she had all their attention. "And can scan for thermal heat signatures to let me know what is in my surroundings. That's how I found you all."

"That's so cool," Rox said.

"There are more things too. I just can't remember them all."

"Very impressive," Teka said.

"Yeah, not bad for an oversized, prehistoric golf ball," Palo laughed. Again, no one else did.

"If you don't mind, Miss Sparrow, I am going to

power down for the night. My battery is at twenty-three percent," Hobbes said.

"Oh, of course," Sparrow replied. "We'll be sure to get you some sun time tomorrow."

"The forecast looks promising," Hobbes said, landing in Sparrow's open hands, the propellers retracting back into its body. "Good night, Miss Sparrow."

"Night, Hobbes."

The light turned off and Sparrow clipped Hobbes back onto her vest.

"I think we better call it a night, too," Teka said again. Rox opened her mouth to speak, but Teka cut her off. "I know you have more questions for our new friend, but you'll have plenty of time to talk tomorrow. It's a long walk."

"About a day," Sparrow added.

"Hopefully less," Palo said, reclining on the ground near the embers.

"Hopefully," Teka replied. "See you all in the morning."

"Good night, Sparrow," Rox said.

"Night, Rox," Sparrow replied.

They all found a place close enough to the embers to keep warm, but far enough away to not burn themselves. Sparrow fell asleep thinking of all the questions she would ask about life in The Stream. She wouldn't have to wait long to ask them.

The night came and went like a flame stomped out with a wet boot and she woke with a start as a thunderclap shook her awake.

FIVE

Sparrow jumped to her feet and grabbed her bo staff from her back, all in one movement. Her leather hat fell off her head in the process. Hobbes jolted awake and tried to fly into the air, but was restricted, due to still being attached to Sparrow's vest. She looked up to the sky for the thundercloud, but saw clear, blue skies. She dropped her head to the family around the charred remains of the fire.

"Sorry about that," Rox said. She held a small metal pan in her hand and bent down to pick up two more off the ground. "These were in our emergency kit and are much heavier than I thought. I think they're for food?"

Sparrow laughed. She did not know what was funnier: being scared awake by some falling pans or someone not knowing what pans are for. She put her bo staff on her back and knelt to pick up her hat. She brushed the dirt off and pulled it tight on her head.

"It's okay. Needed to wake up anyway. Didn't realize I was so tired." She walked around the makeshift fire pit and helped pick up the pans. "And yes, these are for cooking food."

"Oh, I've heard about this," Rox said with a smile. "It's like taking food pieces and putting them together to make something else, right?"

"That is the weirdest way to describe cooking," Sparrow replied. "They don't cook in The Stream?"

"Of course not," Rox laughed.

"You have to eat, though, right?"

"Well, yeah. Remember last night when I showed you this." Rox pulled up her sleeve again and showed Sparrow the triangle-shaped holes in her arm. "All the nutrients you need go in there. You can adjust the levels if you want, but most people just set it and forget about it."

"I've never heard of anything like that," Sparrow said. She had moved closer to Rox and was inspecting the three holes. "Well, I can make breakfast if you'd like."

"We would love that," Teka said. "Maybe we'll learn a thing or two."

"Sure thing," Sparrow said. She walked over to the bags. "Let's see what you've got."

She found seven expired MREs, and some powdered milk. There was not much to be done with such few rations, but she ran back to the creek to get some water, and then boiled it, once she got the fire going again. She made some kind of chili mac. The family seemed well pleased.

"I forgot that food has taste, too," Palo said. "Not just nutrients. Before the VR-evolution, I used to love this amazing pad thai from a local place. Magical Noodle, I think it was?"

"If you think this expired food is good, you should try some of the stuff Mom makes back at the castle," Sparrow said, taking another mouthful.

"The castle?" Teka asked.

"It's where we live," Sparrow replied.

"You live in a castle?" Rox said. "Like from the Middle Ages? That's so cool."

"Oh. No, it's not a real castle. It's a—" Sparrow caught herself. She was not ready to tell these people where she lived. And, if she told them about the tower, it would be easy to find. There were no other towers in the area. "—just a cabin across the lake. We call it the castle because it has some stone on the front."

"I see," Teka replied. "We better get going soon, yes? We've got a long walk ahead of us."

Sparrow took their pans and utensils down to the creek to wash them off. She was just out of earshot, but she thought she heard the family say "flying" and "flaggers" and "dangerous." She brought the clean pans back to the camp and the family stopped talking. Sparrow looked at them for a moment, trying to decide if she should ask any questions to discover their true intent. She decided against it. It was enough for her that she had someone to travel with, and they did not seem like they would harm her, no matter their intent. So, she handed the pots to Rox then said, "Follow me."

She led them back to the edge of the lake. They all gasped when they saw how the sun made the lake shimmer, and how the mountains stretched to the top of the sky above the clouds. Rox could not take her eyes off the lake. She was so distracted she regularly hit her head on low tree branches as they approached. Hobbes was awake and scouting the area for danger in the form of thermal signatures. They had been walking for just over two hours when the lake banked to the east.

"First rule of surviving out here," Sparrow said. "Never travel on the main roads. After seeing you all yesterday on the west highway, I'm surprised you're still alive."

"You were going along the road," Palo said.

"I was flying," Sparrow said in a smart aleck tone. "That's different. There's no way to avoid the wildlife. Wolves, mountain lions, bears. They don't use roads. Could be anywhere. But the Flaggers, they only use the roads. They don't leave the city often, but you can't be too careful." She looked up to Hobbes flying just in front and above them. "Speaking of careful, Hobbes, any enemies nearby?"

"Negative, Miss Sparrow," Hobbes replied. "Present company excluded."

"Hobbes," Sparrow said in a long-drawn-out way.

"My apologies."

The family did not look up or acknowledge Hobbes slight against them. They were still taking in the scenery around them. Rox was walking forward, but still looking back, taking in as much of the shrinking lake as she could. Sparrow realized this would be a good time to learn more about The Stream, since her mother told her very little.

"So, everyone is connected to The Stream?" she asked. The family took a second to respond, after the abruptness of her question wore off.

"Most people are," Rox said. "Except for the Flaggers, of course. And you, I guess."

"Even babies?" Sparrow asked.

Rox looked to her mom and dad to defer this question to them.

"Of course," Teka said. "Why not? Is your baby having trouble learning to speak? Have her talk with a personalized speech bot, any time you like. Need work on motor skills? Build a playpen, no, play world, with puzzles and games designed specifically for your child."

"But, if everyone stays plugged in, how are they born?" Sparrow blushed at the question.

"Science, of course. And technology. It's not difficult. Quite boring though."

"Oh," was all Sparrow could think to say. She wanted to change the subject. "There's an abandoned village up to the west. If everyone can connect to The Stream from their homes, like you all, why did they leave?"

"Oh, I'll take this one," Palo said. "They simply couldn't afford it. Costs a lot to get a self-sustaining energy source set up, you know."

"How do they plug in, then?"

"Oh, right. Forgot about that part. There's a facility way out west. What's it called, dear?"

"The Sanctum at Ravenden," Teka replied. "Bit pretentious, if you ask me."

"That's right. Everyone just calls it Ravenden. Huge facility. Thousands of people with their own tanks." Palo clapped the dust from his hands. "Too civilian for my taste."

"But, when you're in The Stream, you can't tell a

difference," Rox added. "Most people don't talk to anyone else, though. Allybots are personalized for your taste. If they don't make you feel good, just fine tune its parameters. It's easy. Most of the time, you can't really know if you're talking to a human or an Allybot. Not that anyone cares either way."

"Sounds terrible," Sparrow said.

"Rox hasn't begun to tell you what The Stream can do. Maybe tell her the enhancement, dear?" Teka added.

"What do you mean?" Rox asked.

"What color is Sparrow's shirt?" Teka asked.

A slow smile spread across Rox's face, as if she was recalling a distant memory. "Looks dark green to me," she said.

"Really?" Sparrow said looking down at her clothes. "It's pretty red."

"Rox is colorblind, I'm afraid. Born that way."

"But in The Stream, I can see everything just fine!" Rox said, cutting into the conversation.

"That's right, because the tanks are connected to the brain directly."

"This is so much. I don't really understand," Sparrow confessed.

"It's okay," Teka said. "It's all quite technical. You haven't even asked the interesting questions, like what can you do? Who can you be?"

"What do you mean?"

"I mean, do you want to swim to the bottom of the ocean and explore the remains of the Titanic without an oxygen mask or fear of shark attacks? You can do it," Teka's voice rose a few levels. "Better yet, want to see what it was like on-board while it was sinking? That moment exists."

"I've read about the Titanic," Sparrow said. "I know what happened."

"Of course," Teka replied. "But you could feel what happened. The frantic bustle of collective panic. The screams and wails. The frozen air on your cheeks. You can live it, and then it's not just facts about an event, it becomes part of you."

Sparrow's mind was reeling.

"It doesn't have to be only sad things, though," Rox said, breaking Sparrow's trance. "My favorite thing is the Art History Alive server. There are millions of moments that have been recreated so you can experience in full immersion.

Want to float next to Michelangelo while he paints the Sistine Chapel? Done it. Want to sit on the bench while Handel taps out Messiah for the first time? Amazing. Want to read the first draft of Fahrenheit 451, page by page, as Bradbury churns it out from the nickel typewriter in the UCLA library? Pure bliss."

Sparrow kept walking, leading the group, as she worked out the possibilities of The Stream.

"Could I fly in a rocket ship?" Sparrow finally asked.

"Sparrow," Rox replied, "You can fly with Neil Armstrong in the Apollo 11 and walk on the moon with him."

"It would just feel like watching a movie, right?"

"It's real. It's as real as us walking past the lake back there."

"I'm sorry," Sparrow said. She stopped walking and

they stopped behind her. Hobbes hovered overhead. "I can't understand."

"It's okay," Rox said. "We can talk about something else."

"Why don't we walk in silence for a bit, dear," Teka said, putting her hand on her daughter's shoulder. Sparrow gave a thankful smile.

They walked for a few more hours, stopping every thirty minutes or so to take a break. The family had not exerted this much energy in over a decade; a whole lifetime for Rox. The forest was thick leading up to the city, and the hills rolled, blocking the cityscape from view. This caused Sparrow to get lost multiple times. The day trip turned into a day and a half.

As they reached the top of a berm on the second day they could see the shadowed city, darkened by the mountains.

"I don't think we should go into the city at night," Sparrow said trying to hide the tremor in her voice.

"If that's what you want," Palo replied right away. He let out a deep breath.

"Let's all go find some wood and fire stuff, so Sparrow can start us a fire for the night," Teka said. They put their backpacks down and went shallow into the woods. Sparrow gathered some dead leaves and returned to the campsite. It did not take long for her to get the fire going this time. She cooked them another round of chili mac.

"I think it was better tonight," Rox said.

"It was the exact same," Sparrow laughed.

"Tasted better to me," Rox replied.

"Well, thanks," Sparrow said.

They put their plates back in the bags. Teka and Palo were talking quietly and looking at a paper in Teka's bag. Sparrow and Rox were laying back looking at the stars. After a few minutes of silence, Sparrow spoke again. "Can you tell me more about The Stream?"

Rox leaned up and looked at her mom.

Her mom gave her an approving nod.

"Of course," Rox said with a smile. "What do you want to know?"

"I don't know. What's life like in there? What do you do all day?"

"Same thing as you, I'm sure. I still have my studies. Except, instead of opening a book and reading about the first Skylight, Hercules Adams, I get to hold the lantern while standing tall on his horse."

"Do people work, though? Do your parents have jobs? I mean, how do you make money?"

"Most people do, I think. It's different though." Rox paused. "Does your mom have a job?"

"Well, no," Sparrow replied.

"You seem to have been getting by fine without one, too. In The Stream, people get by. There's no life value from work anymore. There's no, 'I'm a teacher. My work is important. Therefore, I am important.' It's not like that. It's more like, 'I'm interested in this thing,' then you can go experience it. People are defined by their passions more."

"So, what are you passionate about?" Sparrow asked.

"Oh," Rox cheered. "Art, of course. Paintings. All eras. It's so interesting to me."

"Why?"

"Because these ordinary people—obviously talented —took pieces of the physical world and said, 'Submit to my will' and created beautiful masterpieces with the raw materials.

I spend most of my time in moments where artists are creating their early masterpieces; moments as they are devoting so much time to learn their craft, but before the recognition has caught up to their efforts, when they are at their highest levels of unbound creativity and lowest levels of pressure.

There's nothing like sitting in the upstairs, dusty loft of a studio in middle America, a hundred years ago, while a painter works on their first great work, while the wood panel floors bend with every step, and a random bathtub sits in the corner." Rox closed her eyes and was transported back to those places.

"Do you ever paint?" Sparrow asked.

"Oh, me? No, no. There's not really any of that in The Stream."

"Why not?"

"I don't know. It's too easy to select a different paintbrush or scroll through thousands of options to get the perfect color. There are no mistakes because anything can be changed after the fact."

"Oh," Sparrow said.

"There's no process," Rox continued, "Which I think is a big part of it. I'm not sure. But no one takes the time to collect an egg, crack it open and just get the yolk, pierce it so the inside yellow comes out, mix it with pigment, and work it to get the right finish so it's not too watery or greasy."

"I had no idea," Sparrow said.

"Things just happen when you want them to. And why shouldn't they?"

There was another long pause. The woods teemed with life as thousands of bugs sung in the moonlight. Sparrow felt one land on her nose. She reached up to flick it away and hit her hand on Hobbes, still tethered to her vest.

That gave her an idea.

"You want process? Go find as many sticks as you can. At least as thick as your thumb."

"What?" Rox asked.

"Just do it."

Sparrow got up and went to the edge of the trees and gathered four or five sticks. She returned to the fire and Rox joined her.

"I don't understand," Rox said.

"Well, last night you said you've never heard of bowling. And tonight you said there's no process. So, we're going to go bowling. Put these sticks facing up in the dirt in a triangle."

"A triangle?" Rox asked.

"Don't tell me you don't know what a triangle is," Sparrow replied.

"We still have triangles," Rox laughed. "I just don't understand how to set them up."

"Like this." Sparrow took one of her sticks and shoved it into the dirt and made the headpin. Then, she took two more and put them behind the first one. It did not take Rox long to catch on. She put three sticks behind the two Sparrow had placed. They teamed up to place the last four sticks behind the row of three.

"We need a ball, right?" Rox asked.

"Got that covered. Follow me." Sparrow stood in front of the head stick, turned her back to it, then took fifteen large steps. She stopped, turned around to face the pins, and drew a line in the dirt. "You can't cross that line."

"Okay, but where's the ball," Rox asked again.

"Here," Sparrow said. She unclipped Hobbes from her vest and handed her spherical robot companion to her new human friend.

"Are you sure?"

"This hunk of metal won't be hurt by a few twigs," Sparrow said. She ran back down to the pins, yelling on the way, "You're up first." She stood behind the pins, waiting to collect Hobbes.

Rox moved Hobbes around in her hands, looking like she was trying to decide if she should roll with her right hand, left hand, or both hands. She shuffled up to the line holding Hobbes in both hands and let it roll.

A small cloud of dirt puffed on impact, but it did not slow Hobbes down one bit. The metal bowling ball was heading straight toward the sticks. They both waited with bated breath. Then, the ball took a slight left turn, missing the headpin, but just clipping the number ten pin on the right side.

Rox cheered. Sparrow clapped.

They heard a buzzing sound like something whirled to life.

Hobbes flew next to Sparrow.

"Excuse me, Miss Sparrow. I am not a toy."

"Oh, come on, Hobbes," Sparrow replied. "I was just teaching Rox bowling."

Rox ran to join them. "Did you see that," she exclaimed. "I got one."

"Good job," Sparrow said. "Usually, you would get another try to knock the rest down, but our bowling ball is being stubborn. Which is typical of this particular model."

"Girls," Teka said from the other side of the camp. "What do you say we get some rest?"

"Just a minute, Mom," Rox replied. She walked over to the nine sticks still standing in the dirt. She reached down and picked up the one that had been knocked down. Sparrow saw her smile as she ran over near her mother and put it in her bag.

"Sorry, Hobbes. She just seemed a bit sad."

"It's quite alright, Miss Sparrow. I did not do much else today, so I'm glad I could be of some use."

"Oh, Hobbes. Don't talk silly like that. It's my fault for not letting you get a full charge back at the castle because I was scared," she apologized. "What is your battery level, anyway?"

"Twenty-seven percent."

"Okay. Can you keep watch tonight and then get some sun tomorrow morning?"

"Of course, Miss Sparrow."

"Thanks, Hobbes."

She put her hands together, like she would to catch water from a stream, but instead of water, Hobbes landed there. She walked near the family and found a small boulder just inside the woods. She set their thermal lookout on the rock, and three legs came out of the holes, normally reserved for propellers, and stabilized the sphere. She patted the top of her companion's metal sphere before returning to the group.

Not much was said before they went to sleep. Teka and Palo put a small paper back in their bag as Sparrow returned. Rox kept telling them about how much fun she had while bowling. Sparrow did not have much to add. She lay under her blanket, watching the stars, and fell asleep, as Rox chatted on about the one stick she knocked down.

The next morning, Sparrow was the first to wake.

Sitting up and looking at their campsite, she noticed Teka's bag was partially open, and the corner of a paper was hanging out. The rush of adrenaline jolted her awake. She could sneak over there and peek while they were sleeping. If they caught her, who knows what would happen. She could not take all three of them with just her bo staff. "But why were they being so secretive with that paper?" she thought. She decided to find out.

SIX

While Sparrow was trying to find her courage, Hobbes' voice squandered her plans.

"Warning, mountain lion detected, point three seven miles southeast of our location. Warning."

The family sprung awake.

"Let's go," Teka said. "If we leave now, I bet we can stay out of its way."

"My suggestion exactly," Hobbes replied.

Sparrow jumped to her feet, pulled on her brown hat, and secured her bo staff to her back. She rolled up her blanket and gave it to Rox. They left the campsite minutes after Hobbes sounded the alarm.

They walked for a short distance in silence before the trees cleared and they were out of the forest, standing in a grassy field. The skyline of the city looked magnified. Sparrow had never been this close to it before. Fear seized her all over again.

"Remind me the plan," Sparrow said. Her voice trembled.

"Try to find a way to connect to The Stream. Ask for a technician to come repair our panels. Go home," Palo said with little emotion.

"There's no way to connect, though," Sparrow said. "Or the Flaggers would have found it by now."

"There's still one place," Teka said. "If we can get power there."

"Where?"

Teka pointed toward the cityscape, singling out one building that looked like three thin buildings combined, with the tallest in the middle. They were linked together with what looked like stitches all the way up.

"That's FerVR," she said. "I used to work there."

"Oh, we're going to FerVR?" Rox said with excitement. "It's blacklisted in The Stream. No info on it anywhere. If you go to Zero City in The Stream, the building just isn't there."

"Why?" Sparrow asked.

"Don't know," Rox replied.

"Then, how do you know about it?"

"People use code names for it. They call it 'The Mountaintop.' No one knows much about it."

"Do you?" Sparrow asked Teka.

"Some," she replied. "Now is not the time, though. We've got a mountain lion on our tail, remember?"

Teka walked ahead of Sparrow and led the group toward the city. As they walked, the grass turned into dirt, which turned into rock, which turned into busted concrete. Small buildings surrounded the city but grew taller the farther into the city they went. Some windows were busted, but not too many. The city looked like it could spring back to life at any moment if given a good reason. The only thing out of place was the overgrown plant life.

Weeds exploded through the cracks in the concrete at every turn. The streets were filled with green overgrowth one or two feet high. Vines overtook the smaller buildings and battled with the bright green moss for total structure domination. Car tires were flat. The only sound was birdsong and the buzz of Hobbes' propellers echoing off the buildings.

Though Sparrow was intrigued and terrified by her first jaunt into the city, the way Teka had dismissed the topic of FerVR did not sit right with her. She decided to bring it up again.

"What did you do at FerVR?"

Teka seemed a bit shocked at this question but gave a faux warm smile before answering. "I worked in the authenticity department. Making sure everything in The Stream was imperceptibly identical to everything in the physical world. Sometimes even improved from how it looked in the physical world." She laughed a little as she continued. "Though, no one called it 'The Stream' in those days."

"Okay," Sparrow said, trying to hide her confusion.

"Wait," Rox said. "Things in The Stream used to not look like they do now?"

"Of course not, dear," Teka replied. "Building a paradise takes time."

"What do you mean you improved things from the physical world?" Sparrow asked.

"Mostly small things," Teka replied. "Walking through an orchard you'll never find a rotten apple. Unless you want a rotten one. We put the nose back on the Sphinx and turned back the clock on the wind damage. Looks like the day it was finished by default, but you can jump to any point in time you want," she explained. "And, no bugs just flying around," she said, as she swatted at a bee. "Nasty things."

Sparrow must have looked confused, because Teka continued.

"We didn't change anything fundamental, if that's what you're thinking," she said. "The virtual world can surpass the physical world in every way, if we'll let it."

"Except for FerVR," Sparrow replied.

"What?" Teka asked.

"You said you didn't change anything fundamental. But FerVR is gone in The Stream."

"That's much more complicated than you understand."

That statement hung in the air.

Hobbes broke the silence.

"I'm going to power down, Miss Sparrow. It is too difficult to get accurate heat signature readings with the buildings interfering, and I need to recharge."

"Of course," Sparrow said. Hobbes flew into her hands, and she clipped it to her vest. She pulled her bo staff from her back and gripped it tightly as she walked.

"How much farther, Mom?" Rox asked. "It seems

like the building is getting closer and that we're not gaining any ground all at the same time."

"We're close," Teka said looking around. "We just need to take 152nd Street down through town."

"Wouldn't it be faster to go up Mercer and cut through King's Boulevard?" Palo countered.

"No, I don't think it would be faster. This is the fastest way," Teka replied. "You just help keep an eye out for danger."

Teka continued leading the group in a straight line with Rox behind her, Sparrow third, and Palo at the end. Now that they were closer, Sparrow could see that the stitches between the three FerVR buildings were hallways connecting the buildings. They were glass tubes with metal banding every twenty or thirty feet. Some of the walkways near the top floor leading to the middle building were broken off. The fragmented glass suspended sixty-some stories in the air.

When they walked across an overpass, completely void of cars, Rox spoke. "It doesn't look like it does in those old movies."

"What do you mean?" Sparrow asked.

"You know, like how the cars are all abandoned in the middle of the road, and they're all piled up."

"I don't know."

"You don't have movies in your forest house? You're old enough to remember before The Stream, though. Didn't you watch movies then?"

"I—," Sparrow hesitated. "can't remember anything before living in the castle with my mom when I was six or seven."

"Oh, I'm sorry."

"It's okay. I think something happened, like an accident or something. I heard my mom talking about in in her nightmares when we first moved to the castle. Anytime I would ask her about it, she would say we don't talk about life before we moved out to the woods."

"That's kind of weird, right?" Rox asked.

"I guess," Sparrow replied. "I've got this scar above my ear, too." She pulled her hat off and lifted her hair to reveal the pink scar about her left ear. "Can't remember a single thing about it."

"Does it hurt?" Rox asked.

"Nope," Sparrow replied. "I usually forget it's there."

That made Sparrow curious about if you could get hurt in The Stream, but before she could ask, they turned the corner and the FerVR building stood in front of them, touching the clouds.

Teka stopped them all at the foot of the building and addressed them. "Well, here we are."

"Now what?" Rox asked.

"We go inside, find one of the old batteries—this building had tons, because we were constantly blowing the fuses—get connected to The Stream, and have the technicians sent to our house."

"Easy," Palo said. "Lead the way."

Teka turned toward the building and took a deep breath before walking toward the revolving entrance. The front had six revolving doors. They were all jammed full of trashcans and food carts to keep them from revolving.

"Spread out and see if you can make one spin," Teka said.

"How?" Sparrow asked.

"Just push on it," Palo replied. They fanned out and Sparrow grabbed the handle of the glass door and began to push. On the other side of the glass were desks, chairs, and computers all in a pile. She was able to revolve the door a few inches.

"Over here," Sparrow yelled. The family joined her, grabbed hold of the bar, and helped her push. They were surprisingly weak but provided just enough extra boost needed to slide the pile of junk around the vestibule and open a two-foot gap into the building. Sparrow was thankful for her training with Hobbes.

The lobby was bright with the sunlight streaming in through the glass exterior. It illuminated the giant circular design etched into the floor. Sparrow remembered something she had never remembered before. She ran up to the deep blue logo filling the floor.

"Wait," she said. "I've seen this before." She took off running up the split staircase behind the welcome desk. The stairs went to the second story and surrounded the perimeter of the room. Once she reached the top, she looked back down at the design and saw a circle with three mountains inside, with the word FerVR above the mountains. Under the circle were the words *Come Alive*. "I know this place," she yelled down to the family. "I've been here."

"Why don't you come back down here," Teka said. "We need to stick together."

Sparrow turned to walk back down from where she

had just ascended. "I've been here before," she said to herself. "Come on, stupid scar. Remember."

But there was nothing.

"I've been here before," she said again to the family when she met up with them in the lobby.

"In The Stream, people say The Mountaintop—" Rox said. "I mean FerVR, provided thousands of jobs for people. Maybe your mom worked here, too?"

"Let's walk and talk, shall we?" Teka said. "The sooner we get plugged back into The Stream, the sooner we can get help to find your mom, the sooner we can go home. Follow me."

They walked around the front desk to a hallway full of elevators. A sign read:

BASEMENT: POWER RESERVES
GROUND FLOOR: LOBBY
FIRST FLOOR: PUBLIC RELATIONS
SECOND FLOOR: ADMINISTRATION
THIRD FLOOR: LEGAL AFFAIRS
FOURTH FLOOR: ALTERNATE ENERGY
FIFTH FLOOR: PUBLIC RELATIONS
SIXTH FLOOR: CAFETERIA
SEVENTH FLOOR: RECREATION

The list went on and on with department names made up of words Sparrow had never heard before. She scanned the list until she landed on the last one:

TOP FLOOR: CEO OFFICE

“Are we taking the stairs all the way to the top?” Palo asked.

“Power, Palo. We need power. Generators. Batteries,” Teka replied. She pointed to the bottom of the sign. “We’re going down.”

They walked through a set of doorways at the end of the hall. Darkness surrounded them. Sparrow could see dark grey stairs leading up and down. The walls were light gray. The handrails were silver metal. The door closed and they were in pitch blackness.

“Hobbes,” Sparrow said. “Stay in idle to conserve power but turn flashlight to low.” Seconds later the metal ball clipped to Sparrow’s vest began to glow a dim white light. It was like seeing the sun through the clouds on an overcast day. It took a moment for their eyes to adjust, but then they started their descent with Sparrow leading the way.

It took longer than Sparrow expected to reach the basement. It was five stories below the lobby, under the parking garage. When they reached the point where the stairs ended, Teka led the group through a doorway and into another dark room. Palo saw a light switch in the dim light and flipped it on.

Nothing happened.

“Worth a try,” he said.

The light glowing from Hobbes was not enough to cover the room. Sparrow could only see the ceiling, not the side walls or the far wall. The floor went black thirty feet in front of them, like they stood on the edge of a wide chasm. Wires and electric cords littered the floor. Tables and chairs had all been flipped on their sides. It looked like a stampede of buffalo had come through.

"Flaggers," Teka said.

"They did this?" Rox asked. Her mother nodded.

"Is this it, though?" Sparrow asked.

"Part of it, yeah." Teka replied.

"I can't see anything," Rox added.

"Me either," Sparrow said.

"Better let me take Hobbes," Teka suggested. "I'm the only one who knows my way around this place, and you don't want to go falling off something. This place is hard enough to navigate in the light."

Sparrow reached for Hobbes, but hesitated. Teka tried to affirm her. "I won't keep it for long. As soon as we find a battery and get out of here, it's right back onto that vest."

Sparrow did not like giving Hobbes up, but she could not think of another option.

She unclipped the metal ball from her vest and handed the glowing sphere to Teka, who led them out into the vast room. Hobbes' light was only bright enough for them to see a few feet in all directions. Tall skinny walls filled her immediate vison and rose into the darkness.

"What're those?" Rox asked, pointing to the walls.

"Those are the batteries," her mother replied. "This whole place used to run on its own power grid. Our solar panel technicians were the best in the world."

"Can we get out of here?" Palo asked.

"Soon," Teka said. "They used to keep old batteries down here."

"Didn't you say those were batteries?" Sparrow said, pointing to the giant walls surrounding them. They were walking between a few, getting farther and farther from the stairs. Glass shards cracked underfoot.

"Those are too big to take upstairs," Teka replied.

"What's upstairs?" Sparrow asked.

"You ask a lot of questions," Teka said.

"I'm wandering around in a dark basement with some people I just met, in the most dangerous city in the world," Sparrow snapped back. "I'd like to know the plan, at least."

"That's fair," Teka replied. "We're going to find one of the old portable batteries they used to keep down here. Then, we're going to take it outside and let it charge in the sun. While that's happening, we're going to head up to my old office and see if there are any salvageable computers left that the Flaggers haven't already looted. We'll use the battery to get it powered on and try to connect it to The Stream."

"Seems like a lot of 'what ifs,'" Sparrow replied.

"I'm open to other suggestions," Teka replied. This time, she stopped walking and turned back, looking directly at Sparrow, who stood unflinching.

"I'll let you know when I come up with something," Sparrow replied, putting her other hand on her bo staff.

"Take it easy," Palo said.

"It's alright, dear," Teka replied. "I would be scared, too, if my mother had left me in a tree."

Sparrow screamed and leapt toward Teka. Before anything escalated, Rox stepped in and grabbed the bo staff with one hand and Sparrow's shoulder with the other.

Teka had already turned back around and continued walking, searching for a battery. Sparrow and Rox stood still as the distance grew between them and the light. Palo passed by and caught up with his wife.

"I'm sorry about her," Rox said.

"We better keep up or we'll get lost in the dark down here," Sparrow replied.

"She's not always like this."

"Okay," Sparrow said.

"I'm serious."

"You know what I think?" Sparrow asked. "I think she knows me from before the VR-evolution."

"What?" Rox said in confusion.

"Yeah," Sparrow said. She continued in a whisper. "I think she knows what happened with my accident and how I got this scar." She pointed to the side of her head.

"That means..." Rox trailed off. "That means she probably knows your mom, too."

Sparrow had not connected the dots that far yet.

"I need to talk to your mom again," Sparrow said in a regular volume. She took off jogging toward the steady light ahead. But before she could reach Rox's parents, an ear-piercing scream echoed off the cold, stone walls.

SEVEN

Teka and Palo were standing still, Teka with her hand over her mouth. Sparrow ran up behind them, bo staff at the ready, to see what caused the scream, but the sight made her lose her focus. She vomited.

It was a dead body.

“Is that your...” Rox could barely speak. “Mom?”

“No,” Sparrow said with a hand over her mouth.

“It must be a Flagger,” Teka replied. “See that square tattooed on the top of her hand? That’s what the Flaggers use to identify each other.”

“Even though they’re the only ones not in The Stream?” Rox asked.

“We’re out here, aren’t we?” Teka replied.

The four were silent for a few minutes as they all took in the sight of the middle-aged woman, skin thin and green, sitting sideways against a door. Her teeth had fallen onto her chest and her fingernails surrounded her on the floor.

"How long do you think she's been here?" Palo asked.

"I've been in most of the tombs in the pyramids and she doesn't look anything like them. She still has some of her skin on and stuff,' Rox replied. "Maybe a few months?"

"Did the Flaggers kill her?" Sparrow asked.

"I don't know why they would,' Teka replied. "I've heard that Flaggers have a strict code of honor within their community. At least, that's how it was when The Stream first launched, and the first people started getting banned." Teka paused and looked back at the body. "That was a long time ago, though."

"Can we get out of here?" Palo asked.

"I wonder if this person was sent down here to look for batteries, too, but got lost," Rox said. "Look." She pointed to a flashlight on the floor next to the deceased woman. Sparrow picked it up and tried turning it on. Nothing happened.

"Hobbes," Sparrow said. Her eyes still on the woman. "What's your battery percentage?"

"Eighteen percent," Hobbes replied.

"How long will the light stay on?" Palo asked.

"We've got time," Sparrow said.

"The faster we get out of here the better," Palo replied. "Where to next?" he said to his wife.

"The deep storage unit is behind that door," Teka said, pointing to the door where the deceased woman was propped against. "We'll have to move her."

"Nope," Palo said. "Not going to do that."

"I can do it," Sparrow said. She walked up to the

body and knelt. She looked into the sunken closed eyes. "I'm sorry for this," she whispered. "Please forgive me." She stood up and found a large pile of plastic wrap, came back, and used it to grab the woman, without touching her directly. She held onto her shoulders and drug her to the right side of the door. She laid her down and spread out the plastic wrap over her. "It's not a proper burial," Sparrow said.

"We don't have time for that," Teka replied.

"We can come back for her," Rox added.

Teka paused for a moment before replying. "Yes. Of course."

Teka led them through the door into a small room filled with little doors. It looked like a morgue. Hobbes' light reflected off the hundreds of silver handles. Teka began pulling the handles, opening the doors of small lockers. She pulled out old telephones and drones. A few bundles of power cords. She pulled a box of micro-USB flash drives from a container and threw them on the ground. They exploded all over the floor. She slammed the door shut and continued to the next unit.

"Are you just going to stand there?" she said to the rest of the group.

"We don't know what we're looking for, Mom," Rox said.

"What do the batteries look like?" Palo asked.

Teka reached deep into an open locker as her husband asked that question. She smiled wide and pulled out a box the size of a small trash can. Wires hung suspended from the end.

"Like this," Teka replied in triumph.

"Great," Palo said. "Let's go."

"Not yet," Teka added. "We need to find a few more in case this one is busted. I don't want to have to come all the way back down here if we find out the circuitry is fried on this one. Everybody keep looking."

The group split to either side of the hallway. Sparrow and Rox to the left, Teka and Palo to the right. Sparrow checked the bottom row of lockers and Rox checked the middle. They hoped the top lockers were empty because there was no way they could reach them. Teka placed Hobbes in the center of the hallway to provide light for both sides, and they began scavenging for more solar powered batteries.

For nearly half an hour, the sound of metal doors opening, followed by disappointed sighs, followed by slamming of doors, repeated in pairs of four. The fruit of their labor was scarce, but enough. They found two more batteries. With three batteries ready to be charged, Palo spoke up.

"Three is enough," he said. "It's time to get out of here."

"You're probably right," Teka replied. "And, if we need another one, we can just send you back down, now that you know the way." Teka laughed.

Palo did not.

"Hobbes," Sparrow said to the glowing ball on the floor. "Lead us back out of here the way we came."

"Of course, Miss Sparrow," Hobbes replied. Seconds after the command, the three propellers emerged from Hobbes' body and lifted the lighted robot into the air. It flew down the hallway in the direction from where they entered. Teka, Palo, and Rox all carried a battery. Sparrow led them, behind Hobbes, with her bo staff drawn.

Hobbes led them out the door, past the deceased Flagger, through the maze of giant batteries, over the floor covered with wires, trash, and technology debris, and finally up the stairs along the edge of the room that lead to the main stairwell. They stopped a moment to catch their breath before walking the second leg of their ascent; up the five flights of stairs to the main lobby.

No one spoke as they climbed the stairs, their pace slowing with every flight. Their surroundings grew brighter as they got closer to the ground floor. Light coming through the lobby pushed through the gap under the door and filled the stairwell on the other side. Sparrow pushed the door open and inhaled a deep breath of the crisp air.

"Will that be all, Miss Sparrow?" Hobbes said.

"Oh, yes," Sparrow replied, still catching her breath. "We've just got to find a computer, then we'll be leaving, and you can charge while we're walking back."

"Of course, Miss Sparrow." Hobbes flew down into Sparrow's hands and she clipped her robot friend back where it had been for most of this journey. She remembered back when she made Hobbes sleep in her room a month ago—no, that was just a few nights ago. No charging occurred and now she had to deal with the consequences.

They walked back through the lobby and exited out of the only accessible door; the one they had entered through. Once they made it through the glass revolving door, the sun flooded the street with light. Teka walked past Sparrow and into the street.

"Which way is west?" she asked. Rox and Palo shrugged their shoulders. They all looked at Sparrow. She looked around to find the mountains, then pointed in the opposite direction and spoke.

"We've got a few hours of sunlight."

"Need to make sure nothing will block them," Palo replied.

"I know, dear," Teka said without separating her teeth.

"How about here?" Rox asked. She placed her battery in the middle of the street. "It's right in the sun, and if I follow the sun down to the horizon, there are no buildings in the way because the street is perfectly west."

"That should work," Teka said. "Open them up like this." She pushed a button on the side of the battery and the top opened, splitting equally into two flaps. She pulled them open and set the flaps flat. The black solar panels looked nearly identical to the way Hobbes charged. Rox and Palo did the same.

"How long until they're charged?" Palo asked.

"Not sure," Teka replied. "But it won't matter if we don't have anything to plug into them."

"We need to find a computer," Rox said to herself.

"That's right," Teka said. "My department had tons. Let's go." She turned and went back through the revolving door before any more questions could be asked. The rest of her family followed.

Suddenly, the sound of metal hitting the pavement filled the street. Sparrow turned in the direction of the sound. A metal trashcan rolled by about a hundred yards away. Sparrow readied her bo staff.

Nothing happened.

She thought about going to investigate, but with Hobbes low on battery and the family inside, she decided not to venture around the city alone. She backed her way into the revolving door and entered the building.

She ran across the lobby to catch up. They had just reached the doorway to the stairwell.

"Which floor is it?" Sparrow asked. Rox and Palo both closed their eyes with disappointment. "Did someone already ask that?"

"Twenty-five," Teka said. She pushed the door open and began the climb. Palo entered next. Sparrow and Rox followed behind. "Turn on that glowing robot," Teka yelled down to Sparrow.

"Battery is almost dead," Sparrow called back.

"Almost is good enough. I can't see a thing."

"Not going to do it," Sparrow called back up. "We'll just count the landings."

"Fine," Teka growled. "Palo, hand me that bag."

Sparrow assumed Palo slid the bag off his back and handed it to his wife, but it was too dark to see anything. The only thing she was sure of was that they had caught up with the parents since she bumped into them on the landing of the second story.

"Watch out," Palo said.

"Why'd you stop?" Sparrow asked.

"For this," she heard Teka's voice. Then, half a second later, she heard a cracking sound like stepping on dried out tree branches. Following the sound was a neon orange glow. It filled the corridor and painted the walls. Teka held the glow stick in her hand. It must have been no bigger than a quarter of the size of Sparrow's bo staff.

"You had that the whole time?" Sparrow asked.

"Of course," Teka replied.

"You made me use Hobbes in the basement, now it's battery is almost dead."

"We found three backup batteries, didn't we?"

"Yeah."

"Well, once we plug in and have help sent, you can use the rest of the power from the batteries to charge your little toy."

Sparrow clenched her jaw and exhaled. Rox must have felt the tension because she put her hand on Sparrow's arm. The two parents continued up the stairs. Sparrow was held back by Rox, until she felt they were out of earshot. The clanking of their shoes on the metal stairs helped drown out their voices.

"I don't know what's gotten into her," Rox said. "She's always nice."

"You mean she's always nice in The Stream."

"Well, yeah. What else would I mean?"

"Have you ever seen her outside of The Stream?"

"I must have," Rox replied. "I'm trying to remember."

"You were born into The Stream, learning to swim the virtual reality current before you could even walk on two feet. That is the only way you've had interactions with your mother. It seems like this is how she really is."

Rox paused for a second, then kept climbing.

They passed the door to floor three.

Floor four.

Floor five.

"There must be something else," Rox finally said.

"What?" Sparrow replied.

"A reason she's acting like this. There must be another reason."

Sparrow was silent.

They climbed the staircase in silence the rest of the way. Every few flights they had to maneuver around some overturned desks or busted office chairs, but it wasn't too hard. The most difficult thing was putting one foot in front of the other. Sparrow's feet grew heavier and heavier with each passing step. She knew the family was struggling even more, because they asked to take a break every seven or eight flights.

Sparrow guessed it had been nearly forty-five minutes by the time they came to the landing with the big number twenty-five on it. They pushed through the door and were met with blinding light. The entire exterior wall was made of glass from the floor to the ceiling.

The room looked like it had been practically untouched since the VR-evolution. Thick coats of dust layered the desks and chairs, but the room was not destroyed like the basement. The only exception was the hallway on the side of the room. It was one of those hallways that connected the two buildings together that Sparrow had seen from the ground as they approached. The entrance, a hole halfway up the glass wall, shaped like an oval cut in half, was completely barricaded with tables, snack machines, rugs, chairs, and computer parts. There was no way through.

"Where does that lead?" Sparrow asked.

"Can't remember," Teka replied. She walked into the open room and looked around. File cabinets built into the interior wall filled a large section. Some of the cabinets were open, with papers tossed around. Teka looked through the labels on the outside of the cabinets, found one she liked, and opened it up. A few seconds later she pulled out a piece of paper.

"This is what we're looking for," she said. On the piece of paper was the picture of oversized sunglasses, but the lens was solid plastic.

"What is it?" Rox asked.

"Don't you know?" Teka replied. "We called it *The Sword of Damocles*. The original headset. Before the tanks or anything."

"So, we find one of these pieces of junk and we can get into The Stream. Got it." Palo said.

"This is where we tested everything," Teka continued. "There used to be hundreds of these here. Spread out and find a few if you can."

Sparrow went to the pile of debris covering the entrance of the hallway. She pulled out small chairs and desks. Wires and bright orange extension cords were strung throughout. She moved to one side of the opening and pulled out another chair and file cabinet, stripped of its files, and could see an opening into the hallway. She crawled through and was able to make it most of the way before the metal legs of a table blocked her path like prison bars.

Starting to get claustrophobic, she backed out, sliding along papers the whole way. She found a torn brochure with a young woman holding *The Sword of Damocles* headset. It was light grey and had a rectangle front with a cord, thicker than her bo staff, plugged into the right side.

"I've seen this before," she said to herself. She folded the paper and backed out of the heap in double time. Once free, she stood up and brushed herself off before surveying the room for Teka. To her left, Rox searched through all the desks in the middle of the room. Palo was shuffling through the file cabinets on the interior wall. Teka opened a pair of double-doors and disappeared inside.

Sparrow followed her.

Photograph in hand.

She crossed the room and turned the corner into what she could now see was a large office. The wooden desk, the size of a car, was overturned. Books were all pulled from the shelves and scattered on the floor. Paintings were ripped and pierced in their frames. The room had been thoroughly sacked. Teka was kneeling on the ground, picking up the scattered books.

"What're you doing?" Sparrow asked. Teka dropped the books. Sparrow thought she saw a tear in Teka's usually cold eyes.

"Looking for the headset," she replied. "I've got this room covered. Go check out the conference room outside and to the right."

"This was your office," Sparrow said. "This was your stuff." Teka did not reply, but Sparrow thought she saw a slight head nod. "Why didn't you take it with you?"

"Why would I?" Teka replied. "These books all exist in The Stream. Better yet, I could have Carnegie read them to me. No sense in bringing them."

"Why are you putting them back on the shelf then?" Sparrow asked.

Teka did not answer.

A moment passed.

Sparrow decided to ask about the photo. She unfolded it as she spoke. "This is you, isn't it?" Teka turned around. She took one glance at it before replying. "Used to be."

"I've seen this machine before," Sparrow said.

"It was only the most popular piece of consumer technology ever created."

"Not in the watch tower, though. I think it was before."

Teka held a book in her hand and slammed it closed before putting it on the shelf. "The headset isn't in here." She made her way to the door.

"I've seen this. Before my mom moved us to the tower. I think it was important to my mom." Teka walked past her and was nearly to the doorway. Sparrow pivoted to keep facing her. "Did she used to work here?"

"Yes," Teka said. "We had thousands of employees. I hardly knew any of them."

"Did you know my mom?"

Teka had crossed the threshold of the door and was

standing in the main room looking back into her old office.

"Yes."

No sooner did the single syllable escape her mouth, a small dart with a red feather pierced her neck. Teka's eyes rolled back, and she fell to the floor.

EIGHT

"That's the last one," Sparrow heard a deep voice in the open room say.

"Thought there was four?" another voice said.

"Three, right?" the first voice replied, getting louder. Sparrow jumped and rolled toward the glass side door. She heard a third voice. It was faint and higher pitched. The woman said, "Four."

Sparrow sat against the door frame. She turned toward the double doors where Teka had just collapsed. She saw two men pick up Teka's body and sling her over one of the men's shoulders. Then, the other one spoke. "I'll check in here. Think she was talking to someone."

Sparrow reached up to grab the door handle and tried to turn it, but it was locked. She tugged it harder, but it would not budge. She turned back and saw that the man approaching her had a long tube up to his mouth. He was walking toward the other side of the room but was almost even with her. The man started to turn toward Sparrow.

CRASH.

Sparrow put the end of her bo staff through the glass door and tiny shards rained all over her. She climbed through the hole in the door before the last piece of glass even hit the ground. When she was through, she saw a refrigerator near the door. She hurried around to the opposite side and pushed her back into it. A red feathered dart stuck into the wall opposite of the door. With adrenaline rushing, she kept pushing the giant white box until it toppled over in front of the shattered door.

Now that the door was covered, it was dark in the hallway. The only other light source came from around a corner ahead. She hurried down the hallway toward the light. Shouts filled the large room behind her.

The concrete was smooth, and this part of the building had not been destroyed. There was no way to go, except forward.

The hallway filled with light.

She heard the voices behind her getting louder. They had moved the refrigerator. Her frantic walking turned into a full sprint. With her bo staff in front like a walking stick, she sped around the corner until she reached a door, with a light shining underneath. The voices behind her grew louder as they echoed off the concrete walls. There was no other option.

She burst through the door with bo staff in hand.

It was the big open room.

It was nearly the same exact scene as when they

emerged from the stairwell, with one grave difference; the three family members were passed out and piled on top of each other in the middle of the room.

Sparrow took a step toward them before realizing why this scene looked familiar. The door she just escaped through was right next to the door to the stairwell. She guessed it had been a private exit for Teka when she worked here.

The voices grew louder. There was no time to save the family, even if she had a plan. She did the only thing she could.

She ran into the dark stairwell.

Before the door closed behind her, she was on floor twenty-four. She heard the door open above her, voices and light filling the corridor.

"Well, go on then," one voice said.

"I'm not going down in that dark hole," said another.

"Neither am I," said the third.

"We've got to bring her back."

"Why? Mydoom doesn't know there were four of 'em."

"Oh, yeah?"

"We'll just bring back the three and get this one later."

"Looked a child to me anyway."

"Right," said the deep voice. "Help me get these three down to the tube."

The door slammed closed, and darkness filled the corridor again. Sparrow waited on the twenty-third floor until it got quiet. The Flaggers weren't using the stairwell she and the family climbed. She assumed they must be bringing the family down another set of stairs. She didn't stick around to find out.

"Mydoom," she whispered to herself. "That's the name I heard on the radio. Must be Flaggers," she said, as she descended the rest of the stairs at a moderate pace, careful not to wear herself out, but, also, wanting to put as much distance between her and the Flaggers as possible.

"Hobbes, lowest light setting."

A second later the metal sphere crackled to a dim glow. It took three floors for her eyes to adjust. Once they did, she passed the sign that had the number seventeen on it. She sighed a bit and kept walking.

"Battery level?"

"Eleven percent."

"We'll grab one of those batteries once we get to the bottom and charge you up."

The green light blinked.

Her pace slowed considerably when she made it to the floors with the single digits. The adrenaline had run dry, and her legs were cinder blocks.

"Save your battery. You don't have to reply," Sparrow said. "Do you think the Flaggers got Mom?" Hot tears streamed down her face.

Floor seven, then six.

"She's better than that, though, right? They couldn't get her. Nothing could."

Five.

Four.

"I don't like being alone."

Three.

"She's still out there."

Two.

"I'll find you, Mom."

One.

She grabbed the bottom of her vest and wiped her face with the inside. A few deep breaths later, she readied the bo staff in her hand. "Okay, Hobbes. Lights out." The near imperceptible glow faded. Light shone from under the door. She put her ear on the door.

Nothing.

Complete silence.

She pulled the door open a crack.

Nothing.

Empty.

She opened the door enough to slide through, then guided it shut.

She checked and double checked all her corners. Still nothing.

With new confidence that nothing was waiting for her, she crossed the lobby, crossed the FerVR logo, and made her way through the revolving door. But, when she made it to the street to get a battery, they were all gone. Someone had been here and stolen all three.

Or was still here.

She took off in a sprint around the corner from where they had approached the building earlier. She did not know any other way and did not want to get lost. She found an alley and ducked inside. She sat against the wall, behind a dumpster.

"Hobbes, wake up. I need you to wake up," she said

as she tapped on the metal exterior. The green light blinked on.

"Yes, Miss Sparrow?"

"They're gone, Hobbes. All of them. Rox, Teka, Palo. The Flaggers got them all."

"Are you hurt?"

"I'm okay," Sparrow replied. "I got away."

"Any sign of your mother?"

"No," Sparrow said. "But, right before Teka was captured, she said Mom worked at FerVR and that they knew each other."

"One second," Hobbes replied. The sound of a small airplane taking off purred inside of Hobbes. "Nothing in the database."

"What?"

"If your mother worked at FerVR before the VR-evolution, I should have that data, but there's nothing there. No record of Dr. Hoodia working at FerVR. And, perhaps stranger, there's no record of anyone named Teka working at FerVR."

"I don't understand," Sparrow said. She pulled her hat from her head and ran her fingers through her hair. "What's going on, Hobbes?"

"Unsure, Miss Sparrow."

"Should we go home? We should go home," Sparrow repeated. "Mom might have come home by now. And I'm not even there."

"The odds of Dr. Hoodia having returned to the watch tower are very low."

"The Flaggers got her, didn't they?"

"Those odds are much higher."

"They used a red feathered dart on Teka," Sparrow replied. "They didn't kill her, even though they could have. Which means, if they did capture Mom, maybe she's still alive too."

"That is a good possibility," Hobbes replied.

"We have to find where the Flaggers were taking them." Sparrow thought for a minute. "I heard one of them say that name again, Mydoom. One of them talked about bringing the family to 'the tube.' What do you think that means?"

"I just did an index for Mydoom," Hobbes replied. "Just turn of the century worms and viruses turned up. But the tube. That can only mean one thing."

"Yeah?" Sparrow said.

"Zero City has a complex subway network system under the city," Hobbes replied. "May I?" Sparrow unclipped Hobbes from her vest and the three propellers extended. Seconds later, Hobbes was airborne. A small flashlight opened from the bottom of the flying sphere and the light flashed on against the side of the dumpster. The light showed an image of veins on a grid.

"That's the subway system?" Sparrow asked.

"Correct," Hobbes replied.

"There are as many tracks as there are streets," Sparrow said. "It'll take forever to search the whole thing. That's like searching the whole city by foot. We'll be too late."

"Is there another option, Miss Sparrow?"

Sparrow held her face in her hands. "No," she replied. "You got enough juice to stay with me? I don't want to go down there alone."

"Of course, Miss Sparrow," Hobbes replied. "Though I might suggest I don't fly, unless it is necessary."

"Right," Sparrow said. She pulled her hat down tight. "But, first, show me where we are on this map."

The map zoomed in on the southern portion of the city. The white gridlines widened, and the blue city blocks filled most of the space. A blinking red dot appeared.

"Old Chinn Alley," Sparrow said. "Zoom out a bit."

Hobbes did. A tendril from the subway line crept into view three blocks north of them on the main road.

"There," Sparrow said. "That's where we'll go in."

"Very well, Miss Sparrow." Hobbes shut off the light and retracted it back into the shell. Sparrow opened her hands and the robot companion landed, retracting its propellers as well. She clipped it back onto her vest before taking a deep breath.

"Okay," she said. "Let's go find Mom."

She pulled the bo staff from her back and used it to pull herself up. The alley was quiet and growing darker. The shadows cast by the surrounding buildings filled the space. Sparrow made her way to the end of the alley and peered around the corner onto the main road. There was no movement at all. A few shops had broken windows, most had vines or some kind of greenery threatening to overtake them. The wind blowing on the overgrown weeds was the only movement Sparrow could see. She cautiously made her way onto the street.

"This is north, right?" Sparrow said, looking down a street longer than her eye could see.

"Correct," Hobbes replied.

"Three blocks north."

Sparrow began walking.

"There should be signs directing you, if they have not been destroyed," Hobbes replied. "By the time computation technology advanced far enough for mobile devices, humans were terrible at finding their way around on their own."

"They carried computers with them everywhere they went?"

"That is correct."

"They needed them?" Sparrow asked.

"That is a great question, Miss Sparrow," Hobbes replied.

"I guess I don't go anywhere without you," Sparrow replied.

"This is true," Hobbes replied. "Though you do not need me."

"I don't know about that," Sparrow replied.

They were still a block away, but Sparrow could already see the place where stairs led underground. The sign above the stairs was filled with words, most of which were faded, cracked, covered in moss, or a combination of the three. Sparrow ran the last block toward the stairs.

She circled around to look over the railing, down into the stairs, to make sure it was clear before going down.

There was no one there.

Holding her bo staff with both hands, ready to strike, she walked down the steps in near silence. The stairs turned on a landing and continued going deeper under the city. The darkness grew with every step.

"Hobbes, a little light?" she whispered. The familiar dim glow emanated from the orb.

She reached the landing and was met with papers, cups, and other garbage piled up against the walls. A thin layer of water rested on the floor causing a splashing noise with every step. The walls had been painted all sorts of different colors and words and styles. Most of it was hard to identify, but the glow from Hobbes illuminated something that was easy to read.

KEEP OUT OR DIE.

These words were painted in crimson red on the sign that hung overhead. The square Flagger symbol was painted beneath the words.

"Don't like that," Sparrow said. She walked under the sign and into a large open room with low ceilings. It was nearly pitch black in there, but she guessed the room's size because her voice sounded hollow and there were no walls in sight. Sparrow kept splashing through the water as she moved forward.

"Now what?" she said to herself, but Hobbes replied.

"Walk forward to the track and turn right. Then, keep walking."

"What is it?" Sparrow asked. "Picking up something with your thermal scanner?"

"No, the concrete is too thick," Hobbes replied. "I am picking up a radio frequency from that area. Unfortunately, I am not equipped to broadcast it."

"It's okay," Sparrow said. "Let's go."

She stuck her bo staff out to keep her from running

into things. The graffiti covered walls stole her attention, so the bo staff saved her from bruised knees multiple times, as the wooden end bumped into overturned benches and trashcans. Concrete pillars filled the room in rows. She weaved around them and climbed over a metal bar onto a platform. She could see the tracks before her. She jumped down into a splash. The water was up to her ankles now. She turned to the left. And screamed.

She covered her mouth immediately, while staring at a large figure in the darkness.

A silver eye reflected the light back onto Sparrow. Attached to this eye was a shell of an abandoned subway car that sat still on the tracks. It was a silver beast in an eternal slumber. Sparrow had never seen anything like it and took it to be a beast waiting for her. She caught her breath and turned toward where the subway car was facing. She splashed forward, keeping her boots below the water with every step, to minimize the sound.

"How far is it?" Sparrow whispered to Hobbes.

"It is hard to say, Miss Sparrow."

"Do you think anyone heard that scream?"

"That is a difficult question to answer as well."

"You're mapping this route, right?"

"Of course, Miss Sparrow."

"Okay, good. It's fine, then. I'm fine. I'll be able to get out easy. No problem."

She walked.

And walked.

The tunnel split off multiple times, but Hobbes told her to keep on the main line. The walls arched over onto the ceiling and moss hung down, dripping into the creek beneath her. Faded paint, from years gone by, filled the subway walls. She heard wings flapping, but they stopped shortly after starting, so she chose to ignore it.

After covering nearly half a mile of track, she struggled to keep her eyes open. She would have sworn Hobbes had reduced the light level to nearly nothing. Exhaustion and the adrenaline crash made her eyelids heavy.

"I think I'm going to take a rest here," she mumbled.

"I do not advise that, Miss Sparrow."

"Just a short—"

BANG!

The sound of a gunshot echoed off the concrete walls of the tube.

It was loud.

And close.

She sped up her walking pace to close the distance on the sound. It came from around the left bend ahead. As she approached the bend, she could see the wall lit with a dancing light. She told Hobbes to shut off the light as she approached the curve.

With no sign of humans, she saw a box of orange light coming from a shaft on the left side of the wall. It was a ventilation shaft, she guessed. She stuck her bo staff between the bars and pried it loose. It came off its rusted hinges easily after that.

She climbed inside.

The shaft was just above the surface of the water, so it had stayed completely dry. The light ahead of her grew brighter and brighter. She slowed her pace as she neared the barred grate on the end of the shaft.

She could hear voices now.

Someone yelling something and then laughing.

She reached the end of the shaft and peered through. Fifty feet below, she saw Rox and her parents flat on the ground. Their hands were bound with extension cords. They were trying to back away from a man with a red flag draped on his back.

He was partially obscured by people standing in groups behind him, so Sparrow was only able to catch glimpses of him. His hair matched the flag and was long, down to the middle of his back. He wore a black bandana around his head, like a headband. He paced back and forth, yelling.

"Batteries. Power. Where?"

The family said nothing. Sparrow scanned over them. They did not appear to be injured. But the man was not done with them.

"You will answer Mydoom, now," he yelled again. Mydoom held up a long, wooden staff, with an emerald rock on the top, and struck Palo across the face.

Sparrow gasped.

She recognized the staff immediately.

It belonged to her mother.

NINE

"Mom," Sparrow said to herself. The man stood with the stick in the air, ready to strike again.

"Who is that?" he asked. The people behind him shook their heads. "How many people were in that cursed building?" No one spoke up. "How many?" he yelled, getting right into the face of one of the younger men.

"I think four," the boy replied.

"Four?" the man asked. "You think four? And how many are here?"

"Three," the boy whimpered.

"Good. Good. They haven't stopped teaching basic maths in The Stream," the man said in a calm voice before exploding. "FIND ME THE FOURTH."

The group of Flaggers split into all different directions. Sparrow looked down with her hand over her mouth. Only the family and Mydoom, the man with her mother's walking stick, remained.

There was not enough room in the tunnel to turn around, so Sparrow started to crawl backwards to get out and find safety, until she heard running footfalls below.

"Mydoom. Mydoom," the man repeated.

"I told you not to interrupt me when I'm interrogating."

"We've got visitors."

"I know this," Mydoom said, pointing to the tied-up family.

"No," the man replied. He turned his back on the tied-up family before continuing. He was facing Sparrow's direction. "From the west."

"Oh, from the west," he said in a loud voice, with no regard for secrecy. "Excellent timing. Tell them I'll be right there." The messenger left. Mydoom turned to the family. "We don't get many visitors down here. Now, we've got two in one day. What a good day." He walked off in the direction the messenger had just gone, mumbling "What a good day," over and over.

Sparrow backed out of the shaft at a quick pace.

"I've got to follow Mydoom," she whispered to Hobbes.

"I must say, there is no one guarding the family at this moment," Hobbes replied.

"This is the first sign of mom in weeks."

Sparrow tried to quiet her thoughts to hear if any of Mydoom's henchmen were on the tracks in the tunnel behind her.

Silence.

She scooted out of the vent feet first. Once back on the tracks, she pulled her bo staff from her back and readied it in her hands. "Lowest light setting," she said to Hobbes. A nearly imperceptible glow emanated from her metal robot. It took her eyes a moment to adjust, but when they did, she saw that the only way to go was forward, following the tracks deeper into the earth.

The tunnel widened slightly, and a sidewalk rose out of the water on both sides. Sparrow jumped up on the right side and shook out her boots.

Every hundred feet or so, she came to a service door in the wall. She tried every metal handle on every metal door, but they would not budge no matter how hard she shook them. After the seventh door she gave up and kept walking. It was not long before she heard splashing down the tunnel.

The splashing grew louder, and a light filled the tunnel.

"Hobbes, lights off," she whispered. The light went off. Her options were few. She contemplated running back to the last locked door and hiding in the cleft, but then what? Once the person passed by, they would see her and that would be the end of that. She thought about running up and attacking, using the element of surprise to her advantage. She did not want to be seen if she could avoid it, though.

As she stood frozen, thinking over her options, the person was getting closer.

As the person got closer, the tunnel got brighter.

As the tunnel got brighter, Sparrow could see more service doors. Specifically, the void where a service door should have been.

It was open.

She assumed it was the door this person had come out of to search this part of the tunnel for her. There was only one problem.

It was on the opposite side of the track.

The distance between sidewalks, across the tunnel, was too far to jump. If she tip-toed through the water to try not to make a sound, it would take too long and the Flagger would see her. On the other hand, if she sprinted through, the splashing would give her away immediately.

"Tube C cleared," a muffled man's voice from the Flagger's radio filled the tunnel. The woman Flagger in her tunnel replied, "Tube A cleared."

It was now or never.

Sparrow shifted her bo staff, so she held the top in both hands. After a deep breath, she took a step toward the opposite sidewalk, stuck the wooden stick into the water and jumped across, using the stick to pole vault the width of the tunnel. She covered the distance in a second and slipped on the opposite sidewalk when she landed.

She managed to slip her way into a low roll and ducked into the door, which led to a series of winding metal stairs, lit only from the woman's ambient light outside the doorway. Sparrow did not hesitate to descend.

There was no other option.

"Light," she whispered to Hobbes. The light revealed only a few flights of stairs. Sparrow made her way down as quickly and quietly as possible. She was two flights down when she saw the bright light pass by the opening of the door. Sparrow stopped on the metal step, and the light passed by and faded away. Sparrow slowed her pace down the last two flights of stairs now that she felt relative safety.

Once she reached the ground floor, there were two archways with hallways leading in opposite directions.

"You're still mapping this path, right?" Sparrow said to Hobbes. "I'm definitely lost."

"I am, Miss Sparrow."

"Thanks, Hobbes." She looked at both hallways for a second. "Turn up the light a little." The glow intensified and Sparrow could see farther down the tunnels. They looked nearly identical as she tried to decide which way to go.

"Look," Sparrow said. She walked into the tunnel on the left and knelt to bring Hobbes close to the ground. "Wet footprints. Going into the tunnel." She ran to the opposite tunnel to see if there were footprints there too.

There were none.

"This must have been the way the Flaggers brought Rox and her family from the building."

"It is impossible to say for sure, Miss Sparrow," Hobbes replied.

"It's the only thing I've got."

She took off jogging down the hallway with the wet footprints. There were many sharp turns.

Left.

Right.

Right.

Left.

Straight.

Then, a long straight hallway with the dancing light at the end.

She sprinted to the end and peered around the door frame. It was the large room she had seen from above. The door Mydoom had just exited was ten steps away from her.

Nearly one hundred yards away, on the opposite end of the room, Rox, Teka, and Palo sat struggling to get free of their bonds. Trying not to be seen, Sparrow sprinted across the ten paces to the door Mydoom had exited.

The ground had a thin layer of dirt, which made her steps silent. When she reached the door, she knelt and cracked it open and looked inside.

Another hallway.

This one had small torches lining the walls.

Sparrow slipped inside. The family hadn't seen her.

Doors filled the long hallway. Every couple of feet was another open doorway. She turned to the first one on her left and peered inside. The doorways were not just open, there were no doors at all. The only thing in the room was a small cot. She ducked inside. After regaining her composure, she stuck her head out of the doorway and looked down the hallway. Nothing was moving.

But she heard something.

A deep belly laugh coming from the end of the hall.

Mydoom.

His voice grew in volume as he made his way toward her. Sparrow ducked back into the room. She could hear him clearly now.

"You'll have to make me a better deal than that," he laughed again. "I found them, so they belong to me."

"We just want the woman," one of the voices said. The flickering light was getting brighter. Sparrow guessed

Mydoom was carrying a torch. He was heading straight toward her. The light grew brighter. Mydoom would be to her room in seconds and, without doors on these makeshift Flagger barracks, would easily spot her in the shallow bedroom.

"Then, treat me like a human being and make me a decent offer so I can get out of here," Mydoom replied. "You think I like living like this? With this scum?" His voice was only a few feet away. "Look there, worthless mutt, staying in bed all day." He was right behind Sparrow now.

She had jumped in the bed and covered herself with the tattered blanket. The bed smelled like piss and bourbon. Facing the stone wall, all she could see was the orange glow on the wall. She tried her best to slow her breathing. "What am I supposed to do with that?" She assumed he was pointing at her.

"Just give us the woman, Carl," the woman behind him said again.

"MYDOOM," he yelled.

"Yes, of course. Mydoom," the woman replied, annoyed.

"You can have the little one," he replied, still standing in the hallway behind Sparrow.

"The Roark requests the woman. Let us take her with us."

"Good luck with that. I took this fancy stick from that bald hag and gave her to my crew." Sparrow's heart sank. "They probably already took her out with the trash."

"You'll regret this, Carl," the woman replied. She

walked back the direction they had come. Mydoom was still standing behind Sparrow. "Worthless suits." He pushed through the door into the open room, and it slammed behind him. Sparrow wept uncontrollably.

It could not be true.

Her mother was smarter than these Flaggers. She would never let them take her. Yet, Mydoom held her walking stick like a trophy. Sparrow curled up into a ball on the bed and held her head in her hands. Her grieving was short-lived when she heard the faint scream of a young girl from outside the door.

Rox.

Sparrow pulled the blanket off and threw it on the floor. Seconds later, she was crouching by the door with her bo staff out. She pulled the door open a crack and looked into the big room. Down at the far end, Mydoom was using the walking stick to poke Rox. His voice carried across the room.

"Why were you in that cursed building?" There was no response. "Why?" he yelled.

Sparrow used that opportunity to slide through the door and close it without being heard.

"Trying to find your way back into The Stream, perhaps?" he continued. "Of course, you are." He paused before continuing. "We all are. We all are."

Sparrow walked toward him a few feet then hid behind one of the burning piles of desks and chairs.

"You all look fresh out of The Stream. All clean and proper. Your hair is practically still wet. What did they pluck you out for? Missed paying your credits by a few days? PLUCK! Out of The Stream."

Sparrow realized this pattern of punctuating every sentence by yelling, so she made her movement on these explosions of anger.

"Maybe you tried to access some moments they don't want you to see? Naughty, naughty. PLUCK!"

She moved forward and dove behind a long metal bench with wood piled under it.

"Oh, maybe you found a way to block all the incessant advertisements. Can't have that. PLUCK!"

Sparrow popped her head up and saw Mydoom kneeling in front of the family. He was only fifty feet away or so.

"It's not right, is it?" he continued with faux compassion. "What gives them the authority to take our livelihood from us? Who decides who stays and who goes? Does not everyone have the right to basic human needs? And, yet, here we are, forced underground to live as rats. No one cares about us. No one wonders what happened to the flagged. They just assumed we deserved it and go on living in their fantasy worlds."

"We're not bad people. We're not dangerous. We're just trying to get home." He stood now, his voice rising with him. "I think you can help us."

Sparrow had an idea.

She unclipped Hobbes from her vest.

"We found your batteries in the road. Too small!" he yelled. "Much too small to connect to The Stream. Don't know much about powering the tanks, huh? Those tanks drain power."

Sparrow whispered something to Hobbes.

"We've got a tank here. Think we've got it rigged up

proper, just don't have any way to power it. Was hoping you'd be more help than that bald woman. Guess I was wrong. I don't like being wrong. Don't like it at all. So, I'll just delete this little mistake and pretend like we never found you. Doubt you'll be missed."

He pulled the stick back to strike Rox but was met with a surprise.

Hobbes.

Sparrow had turned Hobbes loose and now the flying metal decoy buzzed right past Mydoom's head.

"What the—"

TEN

Hobbes flew across the open room. Mydoom ran close behind. He pulled out his radio while running. "We've got a working Class-3 CompBot, with the drone add-on, making its way up to Tube A. Bring me that bot in one piece!" Mydoom yelled. He chased Hobbes out of the main room and up through the tunnel where Sparrow had first entered the room.

Sparrow sprang up from behind the bench and ran over to the family.

"Sparrow?" Teka said.

"How did you find us?" Rox asked.

"No time for that now, we've got to get out of here." Sparrow began untying Rox's wrists.

"That's your mother's walking stick, isn't it?" Rox asked.

"Yes," Sparrow replied.

"I'm sorry," Rox said.

"Help get your mother free," Sparrow said after

setting Rox free. Thirty seconds later, they were all free. "Come on."

Sparrow led the family back to the door that led to the sleeping quarters.

"We have to get out of here," Palo said when they were all in the dark hallway.

"My mom is around here somewhere. I'm going to find her." Sparrow replied. "You're welcome to go back up through the tunnels if you want, but they are crawling with Flaggers looking for a flying robot."

"What he meant to say was, 'Thank you for saving us,'" Teka said. "You didn't have to do that."

"Help me find my mom, and we'll be even."

"Of course, we'll help you," Rox replied. "Tell us what to do."

"Just keep a look out for now. Mydoom was talking to some nice-dressed people back here. They said they were from that facility out west. Said someone named The Roark sent them to get my mom and bring her back to them."

"The Roark," Teka said to herself.

"You know her?" Sparrow asked.

"She runs Ravenden."

"Why would she want my mom?"

Teka did not reply.

They reached the end of the hallway and turned right into a wider, well-lit hallway. Flaming torches hung on the walls. The hallway opened to some kind of atrium with a high ceiling and a large fire in the middle. A sign on the wall had a series of arrows pointing different directions with words scribbled next to them.

Left arrow, FOOD.
Left arrow, TUBES D-F.
Right arrow, BUNKS.
Right arrow, TUBES A-C.
Down arrow, TRASH.

"The trash," Sparrow said to herself.

"What about it?" Palo asked.

"I heard Mydoom say they were taking Mom out with the trash," Sparrow replied. "It's all we've got, unless you want to split up."

"To the trash," Palo added.

Sparrow pulled her bo staff from her back as she led their procession across the lobby. Computer parts were scattered in shards all over the stone floor. The plastic bits crunched under the sound of the four escapees heading for the area labeled TRASH. The fire was a welcome warmth as they passed, but the pleasure was fleeting as they approached another doorway, this one darker than the last.

"Hobbes, low light," Sparrow whispered.

Nothing happened.

She felt around her vest.

Nothing there.

"I forgot," Sparrow replied to no one in particular.

"Make a torch?" Teka said. "Using this junk and that fire."

"It's all plastic," Rox replied. "It'll just melt."

"What're they using to keep it going?" Palo asked.

"Wood," Sparrow replied. "Back in that huge room

where you were tied up, there was wood stacked under a bench. I hid behind it when I let Hobbes go."

"Let's go grab some," Palo replied. They made their way back across the room and into the hallway with the bunks. But just as she was about to turn the corner, someone appeared.

It was one of the women from the FerVR building.

"You," she said standing just outside the hallway. She reached for her radio, but Sparrow swung the bottom of her bo staff up and struck the woman's hand. The woman yelled and took a few staggering steps back into the hallway. The radio fell to the floor. Sparrow kicked it back to the family. This gave the woman enough time to pull two small daggers from her belt. She held the blade in her left hand up, and the one in her right, down.

"Mydoom don't like violence much," she grinned. "Too bad he ain't here, though." She paused. "Too bad for you."

The woman let out a yell and ran toward Sparrow with the blades drawn. Sparrow took a step back, but swung her bo staff at the woman, keeping space between them. Sparrow kept moving her weapon back and forth to keep the woman away.

"Where is my mom? The woman who was here. With no hair."

"Oh, that tramp? Don't care." She swung her blades at Sparrow. "I got bigger problems."

Sparrow pivoted her staff and one of the blades wedged into the wood. They were only inches apart now, the woman looking down at Sparrow.

"Well, not bigger, I guess." She laughed as she looked Sparrow up and down.

Sparrow jerked her staff backward and one knife fell to the ground. She swung the staff right, then left, all while advancing toward the woman. They were in the dim hallway now, still sparring back and forth. Her muscle memory kicked in from the hours and hours of training she had done with her mother and Hobbes.

Jab.

Dodge.

Stab.

Redirect.

Sparrow spun the staff in her hand before using its momentum to crack the woman's temple with the solid-wood end of the staff. The woman hit the ground with a resounding thud that echoed off the walls.

She didn't move.

"Is she dead?" Sparrow heard Palo say behind her. Sparrow waited a moment in a ready stance to see if the woman would rise, but she did not. Then, she threw her bo staff on the stone floor and knelt near the woman. As she got closer, she saw the damage she had dealt. Blood dripped from the woman's split ear. Her eyes rolled back in her head.

She was not breathing.

Sparrow began to shake.

There was no stopping it. She cupped her hands around the woman's head. Tears followed and rolled down her nose into the pool of blood gathering beneath the deceased woman. Sparrow struggled to breathe. She leaned back against the wall of the hallway and wept. She struggled to keep her own head up and used her bloodied hands as assistance. Gentle footprints pattered next to her.

"Sparrow," Rox whispered. "I'm sorry."

Sparrow did not reply.

"Let's go," Teka whispered down the hallway. "We'll find our way in the dark."

Sparrow sat, unmoved.

"I didn't mean to do that," Sparrow finally said to Rox. "I didn't. I promise I didn't."

"I know," Rox said. She wrapped her hands around Sparrow's trembling body. "You were brave. So, so brave, Sparrow Hoodia." Rox waited a moment before continuing. "Can you keep being brave for me?"

Sparrow looked up.

"Walk with me."

Rox helped Sparrow to her feet. Sparrow looked back at the woman she had killed, until Rox took her by the hand and led her out of the hallway. Rox ran back in and grabbed the bo staff, but Sparrow refused it. Palo led them back to the room with the fire in the middle. Once they reached the flames, Palo spoke.

"We won't be able to see without a torch."

"We'll figure it out," Teka replied. "We have to go."

Sparrow stopped walking. She took off her vest, grabbed her bo staff from Rox, and wrapped it around the end. It took about a minute to pull the vest tight around the wooden staff and clip it into place. But once it was on tight, she placed it over the fire. Rox tried to stop her.

"Sparrow, no. You don't have to—"

"This piece of wood can do good, too," Sparrow replied. The cotton vest lit right away. As soon as it caught flame she walked toward the dark hallway. "Let's go."

Even with the makeshift torch, they could not see the end of the hallway.

They walked blindly.

The hallway was narrow but bulged every time they passed a doorway. The doors were all locked, so they pressed on. Five minutes later, the dying fire light reflected off a metal structure.

Stairs.

They hurried to the stairs and started their ascent. The vest was nearly embers now and threatened to fall off the bo staff at any moment. The light it provided had turned to a faint glow. When they reached the third landing, the remaining pieces fell off the charred wooden staff and floated to the ground.

They could still see.

"Look," Rox said, pointing to light coming through the window of a door three stories up. They moved double time up the remaining flights of stairs. Sparrow cracked the door open to survey the area. She saw a wide balcony that overlooked another large room with smooth concrete floors and stone walls. There was hardly any technology debris on the ground. The light looked different too.

It was from the sun.

Sparrow pushed through the door and the family followed. They crouched as they made their way to the balcony. Sparrow peered over the edge and saw the open room with tile floor and signs pointing in all directions. To her left was a track with a lifeless subway train frozen in the tunnel's mouth, and to the right was a wide staircase covered in natural light. There were steps on the right side of the balcony leading down to the open room.

"Why are we just standing here?" Palo asked. He started his descent down the stairs. Teka followed. Rox stayed by Sparrow and whispered to her. "Come on."

"I'm not leaving without my mom," Sparrow said, "and Hobbes."

No sooner did she say the name of her robot companion did Sparrow hear an ominous laugh. The four of them ducked behind the half wall of the balcony just in time, hidden from a band of Flaggers walking up the tunnel opposite of the abandoned subway car. Sparrow looked over the ledge and saw the group being led by the man who owned the laugh.

Mydoom.

One of the Flaggers next to him carried a bag with something inside. Mydoom and the man entered the subway car and the other Flaggers gathered around, looking into the windows. Sparrow could see over the heads of the Flaggers and into the train car. The Flagger with the bag had set it on the ground and left the car, leaving Mydoom alone in the small space. Mydoom grinned as he used the stolen walking stick to poke the bag. He jabbed at it a few times before a small metal robot rolled out.

Sparrow covered her mouth with her hand.

Hobbes propellers extended in a split second and Sparrow could see her flying companion buzzing around the train car looking for an exit. Hobbes bobbed in and around seats and poles in the car, tapping against windows and doors, but nothing would budge. Mydoom laughed hysterically and said something, but Sparrow could not hear it.

Then, he started swinging.

The walking stick was being abused by this act of desecration. It had been used to protect, but now, in the wrong hands, to destroy. Mydoom gripped near the bottom of the staff and swung the emerald studded rock end through the air like an axe. The space was tight, but Hobbes was able to maneuver clear of the attacks.

After dodging a series of swings, Hobbes began to glow so bright Mydoom covered his eyes for a moment. Hobbes used this distraction to home in on the pinky finger now shining with bright artificial light.

It happened so fast.

Hobbes flew close and used a propeller to slice off the tip of Mydoom's left pinky finger.

Mydoom roared.

He grabbed his wounded hand with his other. Sparrow could not hear the exact words being said, but she was sure Mydoom was cursing something ugly at Hobbes. Sparrow realized she had a smile on her face as the little bit of vengeance filled her.

It did not last long.

Hobbes had flown out of reach of the staff and was gearing up for another attack when the mood changed.

Mydoom tucked his bloodied left hand under his right armpit and reached into his belt with his right hand. A moment later, he pointed a dull metallic gun at

Hobbes, pulled the trigger, filling the room with a muted gunshot.

Hobbes crashed to the ground of the subway car.

Sparrow collapsed with her back to the half-wall.

Sparks jumped out of the hole in Hobbes' metal exterior.

Tears streamed down Sparrow's face.

Her friend was gone.

The dried blood on her hands came back to life with the new tears.

"We're going," Teka said.

"We can't leave her here," Rox replied.

"Did you see what just happened, Roxana?" Teka replied. She grabbed the arm of her daughter. "We can't do anything against a gun."

Rox tried to touch Sparrow's shoulder but was pulled away by her mother. The family crouched down and made their way up the wide staircase opposite of the train car. The Flaggers, still mesmerized at the events that had just taken place inside of the subway car, did not notice the family escape.

"I'm sorry, Hobbes," Sparrow whispered. "I'm sorry, Mom."

She collapsed onto her back. Another wave of tears crashed over her. She took off her hat and covered her face with it. "I need you, Mom." she whispered. She repeated this over and over in a trembling voice.

A few moments later, wet footsteps sloshed down the wide stairs where the family had just escaped. Sparrow sat up to see if it was one of the family members. When she peered over the ledge, she saw a Flagger, soaking wet from the waist down, running toward the group. Sparrow looked the other direction and saw Mydoom walking back down the tunnel, holding a sack with Hobbes' corpse in one hand, while a Flagger wrapped a cloth bandage around his other. The group of Flaggers followed behind.

"What did I miss?" the wet Flagger asked the group as he approached.

"Not now," a fellow Flagger replied.

"Petya?" Mydoom called back to the person who just joined the group. They were nearly in the tunnel now and out of visual range for Sparrow. "That you?"

"Yes, Mydoom," the wet Flagger replied.

"Talk to me," Mydoom replied.

Petya walked to the front of the moving procession and out of view of Sparrow. When the last Flagger was out of sight, she grabbed her hat and bo staff, and hurried down the stairs toward the tunnel. She could hear the chatter, but it was growing weaker. When she made her way to the edge of the tunnel, she peered in and could see Mydoom's red hair leading the group. His voice echoed off the tunnel walls.

"Where is the bald woman?" he asked.

"Ain't it obvious?" Petya replied.

"Do you think I want to play games right now?" Mydoom raised his voice. "We've got a buyer. Will pay real good. Bring her to my quarters."

"That's going to be a problem, Mydoom, sir."

"Bring her to me."

"We dumped her. Wrapped her in the flag and took her for a swim. Great River swallowed her all up."

Sparrow let out a whimper as the realization kicked in. It echoed off the walls of the tunnel. A few Flaggers looked back but were jolted to attention with Mydoom's response.

"You idiot," he said before smacking Petya across the face with his good hand. "Find her."

"Yes, sir, Mydoom, sir."

ELEVEN

Sparrow sprinted up the wide steps and out of the tunnels. She wept loud and uncontrollably as she ascended. The sun, shining just above the mountain tops, was now beating on her face. There was a platform above ground that looked nearly identical to the one below. She ran across the faded concrete and up to the edge of the platform, sobbing the entire way.

"Mom,' she repeated over and over. "Mom. Mom. Mom."

She jumped down off the platform and onto the tracks. One path led toward Zero City: the other away from the city. She turned her back to the city and ran as fast as her legs would carry her. Spit fell from her open mouth. Tears blurred her vision. She ran for ten minutes straight, slowing her pace with every step. The track rolled over the hills and led to a field filled with train cars. She slowed to a walk.

"Not Mom. Not you, Mom. Not you," she said. A cool breeze swept across the hillside and found its way up her untucked shirt, sending chills in every direction. She barely noticed.

"I can't. Alone. I can't be—without—Mom."

The sun was now partially blocked by the highest peak. Few clouds filled the sky.

"Nothing—to—do."

Sparrow was approaching an abandoned train yard. She stumbled into the yard, her eyes swollen.

"Can't—go—on—Mom."

The track she walked led her next to a rust-brown car. She pulled on the handle with no expectations. It slid open.

"I'm—sorry..."

She used the last bit of her strength to climb inside and slide the door shut. She collapsed without noticing the damp and fecal stench. She closed her eyes and one last tear streamed down her face and onto the train bed.

"I miss you, Mom," she said faintly.

There were no plans on leaving the train car.

Until the voice spoke from the darkness.

"Well, hello there."

She shot up into a sitting position.

"Heard you talking about your mom," the old raspy voice continued. "She die? Sorry to hear that if that's so."

There was only silence in the train car.

"Don't want to talk to the scary man on the train?" he laughed a little. "I understand. Just thought I better introduce myself if we're going to share this coffin."

Sparrow heard some friction followed by a small flame. It touched a small metal can and a blue flame glowed, filling the train car with dim light. The man in the corner was bald and had a long grey peppered beard. He wore an oversized red sweater, but his legs were what caught Sparrow's attention. They were wrapped in a blood-splotched lime green bedsheet. He blew out the match and continued.

"If I had friends, they'd call me Trax."

Something sparked in Sparrow's memory. Her gaze snapped away from the man's injured legs.

"Trax?" she managed to mumble.

"That's right."

"I've...heard that before."

"I doubt that."

"You have a radio?"

"'Course I do."

"You were asking for help. Couple days back?" Sparrow asked.

"And every day since." When Sparrow kept silent, Trax kept the conversation going. "You musta heard it and came to help me, then?"

"I—," Sparrow did not know how to answer that question.

"It's okay. Don't expect no one to help old people. 'Specially old people they don't know." He paused again. "I'm Trax by the way. Did I already say that?"

"I'm Sparrow," she replied. "Is Trax your real name?"

He let out a hoarse belly laugh.

"Of course, it ain't," he could not hold it in. "I just like it." He continued without skipping a beat. "Your real name Sparrow?"

"Yeah," she replied. "What happened to your legs?"

"Leprosy."

Sparrow scooted back against the wall of the train car. Trax belly-laughed again.

"I'm just messing with you. Leprosy ain't no joke, though. Very serious. But that ain't what this is. This is the result of getting ganged up on by a pack of stray hounds."

"Dogs did that? How? I thought dogs were nice."

"You ever seen a dog in real life?"

"No."

"They're nasty creatures. Full of wild instinct. If a dog wants to turn on you, there ain't nothing you can do about it. Sure, cats can turn on you and scratch you up, but you ever seen someone get their legs filleted and lose all walking ability by a cat attack? No, ma'am. Only those dirty dogs are capable of a mess like this. Don't trust 'em."

"Are you going to be okay?"

"That's a good question right there," Trax replied. "Lucky I found a first aid kit over in some village on the way here. Thought it might come in handy. That was before the attack. Had some rubbing alcohol in it, so I think I got it all cleaned up. Might get infected though. Don't matter much anyway."

"What do you mean it doesn't matter?" Sparrow asked.

"Not going to be able to do anymore walking for a long time. Don't have anywhere to walk to anyway.'

"What about your family?"

For the first time, Trax did not have anything to say.

"Oh, I'm sorry. I didn't know," Sparrow apologized.

"They ain't dead," Trax replied. "Might as well be, though."

"I don't understand."

"Back when the VR-evolution hit, we did just like most everyone else and sold all our belongings and bought our tanks in one of those big facilities they got dotted all over the country and plugged into The Stream. I didn't like it much, nothing beats God's green earth, but the whole family went bananas over The Stream, so I stayed to be with them.

"Didn't take long, though, for them to go and do their own thing. I never saw them. Can't hardly recognize anyone in there anyway." Trax paused before continuing. "All this technology, we could have gone on vacations to the moon or the Middle Ages. Breakfast on the Hindenburg. Dinner in the Amazon. But we didn't do any of that. Couldn't even get them to return a message. So, I left."

"Just like that? You left The Stream? The facility?"

"Wasn't easy," Trax replied. "Learned why they call it Ravenden. Bunch a' vultures running it."

"Ravenden," Sparrow repeated. "That's where those people were from who wanted my mom."

"It's the only facility 'round these parts."

"When you left, did you notice anything out of the ordinary? Anything wrong?"

"Hard to tell," Trax replied. "The headset is the last thing they take off. They took out my food tube first," Trax showed Sparrow the triangle scar. It looked just like the one Rox had. "Then, they pulled me out of the tank, not trying to be gentle mind you, stripped my haptic suit off and put a thin robe over my shoulders, and walked me through the facility, all while a message is playing, showing how all of your friends and family will miss you." He paused before interjecting, "Load of bull, that is." He continued. "Then, they take off your headset, but you're already outside. Didn't see anything unusual."

"Why would they need my mom?" Sparrow said to herself. She tucked this question away to be answered another day. "So, you came over here?"

"What?"

"After you left The Stream, you came to Zero City?"

"Oh, no. Not at first. Went north. Spent almost a year up there. Got real cold, though. Too cold for my bones, so I headed back south and ended up around here."

"A year?" Sparrow asked. "You've been out of The Stream for a year?"

"That sounds right."

"Your family must think you're dead."

"Probably don't even know I left," Trax countered. "Anyway, couldn't go back even if I wanted to, with my legs all a mess."

"I'm sure they're missing you," Sparrow replied.

"That's mighty nice of you to say. Thank you," Trax replied. He turned the conversation onto Sparrow. "What about you? If you ain't here to rescue me, what're you doing?"

"It's too long a story," Sparrow replied.

"Does it look like I'm going anywhere?" Trax gestured at his legs and chuckled a little. "Unless you don't want to talk about it. I understand."

"I was just looking for my mom. She's been missing for about two weeks."

"You don't live in The Stream?" Trax interrupted.

"I live—lived—," Sparrow paused and sighed before continuing, "—out by the lake, in a tower in the woods with my mom."

"There's a lake 'round here?"

"Reelfoot Lake."

"Does the fog rise up off it in the early morning sunrise?"

"Umm, yeah," Sparrow replied, a little confused.

"Could you take a little boat out there and let the waves bob you up and down all afternoon?"

"If you wanted, I guess."

"Sounds like a nice lake," Trax replied, before snapping back to reality. "How about that. Here I thought the only people not in The Stream were those filthy Flaggers." Sparrow was in no hurry to go on with her story, but Trax urged her on. "I'm guessing you didn't find your mom, then?"

Sparrow spent the next twenty minutes telling Trax about Hobbes, her paramotor, Rox and her family, their trip to Zero City to find a way for the family to plug into The Stream and to find Sparrow's mom. She told him about the family getting captured, about going into the Flaggers' subway dungeon, and rescuing the family, about the walking stick, the people in the suits looking for her mom, and Mydoom getting his finger cut off (Trax laughed for a solid minute at that part).

She continued, telling him about Hobbes getting shot (the laughing stopped abruptly), how the family left her, and that she overheard the Flaggers say they killed her mom by tying her up and throwing her in the river. She told him everything, except for the part where she killed the Flagger.

"And now there's nowhere for me to go. I'm just going to get in my paramotor and fly away," Sparrow began to weep again. "I'm all alone."

"Well," Trax replied, trying to sound light without being disrespectful. "I know I'm not much, but I'm still somebody. And I'm here, ain't I? You're not alone."

Sparrow's weeping turned to sniffles.

"I know we just met and all, but after hearing everything you've been through, it doesn't sound like you're ready to fly off into the sunset yet."

Sparrow composed herself a bit at the comforting words.

"You know the worst part of leaving my family?" Trax asked her. She assumed it was one of those questions that does not need answering and the person will just keep going, but Trax waited in silence. Finally, Sparrow realized he was waiting for her to reply.

"No," she muttered.

"Not being able to say goodbye." Now Trax's voice began to tremble. "I couldn't get ahold of any of them in The Stream. Couldn't find them in that cursed place. Too big." He was barely able to get through the last part. "Even after my demersion, I knew their physical bodies were in the tanks right next to me, but I didn't get to say goodbye. I didn't get to say anything."

"Demersion?"

"That's just what they call it when you get out of The Stream for good."

"Oh," Sparrow replied. Her mind raced back to her last interaction with her mom. "I told my mom to bring me back some new books if she found any," Sparrow paused. "Didn't get to say goodbye either."

"It's not too late for you," Trax replied. Sparrow's face was downcast. Trax noticed and continued. "You said they put her in the river, right? It's slow moving. Go find her and give her a proper burial. Say your goodbyes."

"I don't know—"

"I know it sounds a bit morbid, but so does living the rest of your life with regret. You can do it. You're one of the brave ones. I can see it in your eyes."

"Mydoom sent some of his Flaggers after her body, too."

"You said you got a flying machine, right?"

"Back at the tower."

"Don't let those nasty Flaggers get their hands on her. She's your mother, ain't she?"

"She is."

"And, you want to say a proper goodbye, don't you?"

"I do," Sparrow's voice grew in volume.

"Then get out of here and go make peace. That opportunity don't come too often."

She felt the adrenaline running through her veins. She stood in the train car and pulled her charred bo staff from her back. She turned to the door and grabbed the handle but paused. Letting go of the handle, she turned back toward Trax and knelt next to him.

"I can't leave you here."

"Oh, stop that. I'm an injured old man. I'll just slow you down. And, you don't even know me." He laughed. "You just promise me you'll spend one morning out on that lake for me and that'll be just fine."

"Thank you, Trax." A tear rolled down her cheek. "You saved me."

"No, ma'am," he said shaking his head. "That's too much."

"I'll come back for you. Stay well."

"I'll do my best, Miss Sparrow."

She squeezed his hand at that name. She was thankful for the friends who had helped her be brave. There was no doing this alone. But the time came for her to leave. She rose to her feet and slid the train car door open. Light blinded them both. After she adjusted, she jumped down into the rocks.

Looking back into the car, she spoke to Trax, "I'll be right back."

Then, she slammed the door shut and took off running south.

The sun had not fully set, but it was close. The radiance was dulled by a cloud-filled sky. Dozens of lifeless train cars filled the yard around her. The air was a bit colder now that she was without her vest. The small rocks smashed under her boots like wet sand as she ran between cars. She held her bo staff in her right hand as she sprinted away from the train yard. Away from Zero City.

No sooner had she escaped the train yard did she feel a cold splash on her face.

Then another.

A thunderclap echoed off the mountains.

"No. No," she begged, thinking about the difficulty of flying her paramotor in a storm, but mother nature played no favorites.

The drops became more frequent.

Gravel turned to grass as she entered the hills. Her feet slowed as she encountered grass up to her shins. She stomped flowers and weeds with ill concern. The wind threatened to blow her hat from her head, so she sheathed her bo staff, clipped the chin strap, then re-equipped the staff; all without missing a step.

"I'm coming, Mom," she thought to herself. "I won't let them have you."

Rain mixed with tears as she ran.

With blurred vision, she could see the edge of the forest ahead.

"I'm coming."

A flash of light streaked across the sky, followed by a splintered crack. She jumped at the sound and looked up. The clouds had grown more ominous and blocked more of the waning daylight. The rain fell harder as she entered the forest.

The rain pattered off the leaves like an organic orchestra. Thunder boomed every few minutes. Sparrow struggled to keep the rain out of her eyes. Her clothes were soaked and her boots full of water. She did not stop running.

After over an hour of running, the edge of the lake was in view, but it looked different than she remembered. At the next clearing, she looked up at the mountains. They were bigger than usual. She realized she was farther east that she thought. Going up to Zero City, they had traveled up the west side of the lake. Now, Sparrow was running up a thin path between the foot of the mountains and the lake on the east side of the lake.

"It's okay," she thought to herself, still running. "Maybe this way is faster. The storm will slow the Flaggers down, too."

She had been running for another half hour when the path opened to the once peaceful lake, and she thought about her friend Trax. "I'll bring him here when I get back. He'll love it." Sparrow wore a partial smile at the thought of bringing Trax to the lake. Despite the circumstances, and frigid rain, it felt good to think about doing something good for someone.

The eastern path came to an end and was replaced with overgrown forest. Small trees and tall weeds blocked the path. Large rocks extended out into the water, blocking the path completely. She could get through, but at a quarter of the pace she was making on the trail. Her clothes were already soaked through, sticking to her skin, so she did what any desperate person would do. She secured her bo staff on her back and jumped into the ice-cold lake.

She remembered her mom telling her how dangerous it is to swim when there is lightning, but there were no other options. When she entered, her first thought was regret. The freezing water paralyzed Sparrow immediately after entering. She struggled to keep her head above the surface. Her limbs begged to retract in tight to her body. Her feet kicked, keeping her head up and her blood flowing. This kept her moving the right direction, toward the tower.

Her fingers regained their feeling. Then, her hands and arms. She could move her toes in her boots. The water had not changed temperature a degree, but her body was getting used to the cold water, so she was able to loosen up a bit.

Which meant she could swim faster.

After reorienting herself, she reached forward, hand over hand, and swam full strokes toward the southern bank. The rain droplets fell steady on the surface of the lake, creating tiny water eruptions every few inches. The wind rushed over the lake, making the cold water on her face feel even colder.

It would be easier to stop swimming and rest here, letting the lake be her new home. There was no way she was going to find her mom before the Flaggers. Not at this pace. Not with all the obstacles; physical and mental. Besides, there was something poetic about her final resting place being in the water, just like her mom. Sparrow was pretty sure the Great River flowed into Reelfoot Lake, so they would finally be together.

The day turned dark as Sparrow's eyelids dropped. Her arms and legs kept moving, swimming on autopilot, while her mind began to shut down. She slipped into a dreamscape, where she was sinking into the lake. Drifting down far below the surface like an angel, hair floating free from the bonds of gravity. No longer cold. Weightless in the depths and seeing someone floating toward her.

Her mom.

Glowing in celestial brilliance.

With arms wide, her mother approached, smile on her face, whispering, "Come to me, my Sparrow girl. Don't give up."

Sparrow swam. Her arms and legs working without restraint to reach her mother. The figment getting shimmering closer and closer. Sparrow reached out and grabbed her mother's hand, but it squished like sand. Sparrow, now only a few feet from her mother, tried to close the gap but was unable to move her arms. Her mother floated away from Sparrow back toward the darkness. Sparrow tried to scream but was suffocating.

Her mother repeated, "Don't give up," as she floated away and was gone.

Sparrow gasped for air.

TWELVE

Her face was caked with sand. Her arms were over her head, legs kicking in the shallow water. She had washed up on the beach. Pushing herself up, she pulled her bo staff from her back to help steady her tired feet. The sand was easy to wipe from her face with a splash of lake water. There was no reason to waste time getting the sand off her clothes. She looked up and could see The Castle lifting its head above the treetops.

Stumbling, she started running again.

The sand turned into grass as she made her way into the forest.

Weaving in and out of trees, she made her way with a newfound spring in her step. The rain was still falling as the storm raged on, but she did not want to let her mother down. Even in death. Nothing would stop her.

Not even the angry growl from the surrounding forest.

She slowed her pace, surveying the area in the

direction of the growl. A second later, she heard a thumping, growing in intensity, and the sound of branches cracking. Then she saw it.

A giant brown bear sprinting toward her.

She started sprinting again.

The grizzly was gaining on her. She knew she could not outrun it, so she ducked behind the biggest tree she could find. The bear slowed its pace and sniffed the air. It walked toward her. Unable to move, Sparrow readied her bo staff, but hoped the bear would pass her by.

She was not so lucky.

It roared around the tree, it's head above Sparrow's, even while standing on all fours. Before it could lean back on its hind legs, Sparrow spun the staff in her hand a few times to gain momentum, then smacked the bear's face with a downward blow. The bear was stunned, but Sparrow did not stick around to see how it reacted next.

The bear was not injured by the attack. Seconds later it resumed its pursuit, only this time it was able to catch up much faster. Sparrow could hear the heavy footsteps behind her. She looked back, just as the bear was about to take a swipe at her, and rolled on the ground to the left, dodging out of the way.

The bear was agile for being such a large creature. It slowed and turned with Sparrow. Still on the ground, she tried to smack the bear again, but this time it swiped toward her first. She was able to lunge her body out of the way, but the bear struck Sparrow's left hand. The claws ripped through the tendons and crushed the bones in the back of her hand. Her fingers went limp. She screamed.

The bear growled again, taunting her, now that it had made an attack. Sparrow was not ready to surrender yet. She shifted her grip on the bo staff, so she held it like a javelin and jammed it in the bear's open mouth. The beast roared with pain and bit down on the wooden staff, causing it to split in two, half in the bear's mouth and half in Sparrow's hand. The broken end was sharp and splintered. Sparrow saw this new opportunity as her last option. She jammed the splintered half into the bear's leg. The leg immediately gave out, making the bear furious.

Sparrow scampered to her feet, her adrenaline rushing, and headed for the fire tower.

Her left hand was throbbing now. She cradled the limp red mass against her stomach, her light red shirt turning crimson. The rain did its best to keep the blood clean from the wound. Sparrow was trying not to think of the stinging pain as she looked for any sign that she was close to the tower. Then, she saw it.

Lincoln's Trail.

She used the last of her strength to turn the corner and sprint up the path. Once she reached the end of the trail, the forest cleared and The Castle stood as a mighty fortress in the storm.

Sparrow fumbled at the lock with her good hand, opened it and started her climb. The tower swayed ever so slightly from the storm. As she got above the trees, she could see that the storm filled the whole flat lands, with grey storm clouds as far as she could see. She remembered Hobbes' warning about flying in bad weather.

What choice did she have? It was her only advantage

against the Flaggers, who had a head start, but were traveling by foot. But how much battery did it have left? She could not remember if she had plugged it back into the generator after the last flight. She was nearing the top now and had forgotten about her hand.

Finally, she emerged on the top deck and ran around the outside of the tower to the storage unit that held the paramotor. She reached out with both hands to pull the double doors open but screamed in pain when her mauled hand refused to pull. She was able to get the doors open with her right hand but knew it would be nearly impossible to fly with only one hand. She searched the storage unit for something to protect her injured hand.

Wadded up in the corner, she found a blue wool sweater. It was her mom's. She couldn't bear to use it as a bandage. Instead, she unbuttoned her long sleeve shirt, yanked it off, then pulled on the dry sweater. It smelled like wet leaves. She wrapped the long sleeve shirt around her hand a few times before tying it tight. It would have to do.

The parachute was wadded up and stuffed into the storage unit. It took Sparrow a few extra minutes to untangle the cloth and lay it out on the deck behind her. She felt the urgency as she thought back to how long it had been since the Flaggers set out searching the river. "The odds are pretty good that they already found her," Sparrow thought. She needed to make up some time.

Could she take off from the roof?

That would save nearly twenty minutes of descending down the stairs, through the gate and then out into the open field. A ground takeoff was difficult enough, getting enough speed to get the parachute to catch. And, on the ground, if you had an unsuccessful launch, you just turned around and tried again. That would not be an option from the roof.

There were other things to worry about first.

Like the motor.

Sparrow lifted the motor and fan blade off the hook with her right hand and set it on the deck floor. Then, she turned around and backed into the harness, crouching down, and did her best to pull it tight, using only one hand. She stood up with the paramotor rig on her back, balanced herself, then reached down and grabbed the parachute.

The deck was slick as she raced around the three corners and came to the door of the castle. She used the key around her neck to open the door. Once she turned the handle and opened it a crack, a gust of wind forced it open. She rushed inside and closed the door, locking it again. No time was wasted as she ascended the ladder to her loft. Rainwater dripped onto the floor beneath the ladder.

Once in her room, she slid a wooden panel aside and was greeted by the raging storm again. She was about to unlatch the window when she saw her two other bo staffs standing up in the corner. The memory of attacking the Flagger woman under the subway sent chills down her spine. She hesitated to grab a new staff, for fear of repeating the same dreadful deed. But what if she needed to protect someone else again?

She grabbed the staff, attaching it to the paramotor,

knowing that she would need to be more thoughtful if she was forced to attack again.

Unlatching the window, the wind caught it and pulled it open. Tilting her head down, she pulled herself onto the roof. The wind temporarily subsided, leaving the roof relatively still. Rain still fell in sheets. The metal roof was much slicker than the wooden deck, but the incline was not as steep as Sparrow expected.

She used the momentary lapse of wind to connect the parachute to the paramotor. She clipped carabiner after carabiner onto the metal rig. Some of the cords might have been twisted up, but there was no time or the space to get them straightened out. Sparrow reached her right arm behind the left side of her body, trying to find the pull cord. Her fingers tapped the plastic T- shaped handle before grasping it fully.

Sparrow closed her eyes and prayed there was enough juice left to start it up. She pulled the cord.

Nothing happened.

"Come on," Sparrow cried into the storm. "Just one more time."

A ferocious gust blew up from the south. Sparrow stumbled forward, slipping on the ice-like metal roof. The fan blade and motor strapped to her back threw off her equilibrium causing her to fall to her knees. The parachute threatened to fill with wind, which would pull her off the roof with no hope of cutting it loose. As she slid dangerously close to the edge, she was able to extend her right leg and wedge her heel into the gutter of the roof. She waited for the wind to die down before trying to stand again. The parachute stayed closed.

When it finally ceased, she used the bo staff to help her regain her footing, then climbed back up to the highest point of the fire tower, dragging the parachute behind her. Once back in position, she reached for the ripcord again. "Come on," she yelled. A sound like thunder echoed behind her as the paramotor roared to life.

She tilted her weight backwards to counter the giant fan on her back. She reached up and grabbed the cords connected to the paramotor frame via carabiners. The pain throbbed in her injured left hand when the tension of the parachute filling with air pulled against her in the opposite direction. She found the throttle with her right hand and pressed the button, causing the motor to growl to life. The timing had to be perfect. The parachute needed to be full enough to support her weight, but not too full to pull her backwards off the roof. Once the chute had filled enough that the possibility of it collapsing was reduced, she needed to hit the throttle and take off running at the same time. Her runway was only about thirty feet, about a quarter of what she was used to on the ground.

There was no time to think about that now. She felt the tugging from the parachute filling up behind her. Inhaling a deep breath, she took off sprinting, holding down the throttle button as hard as possible.

Running.

Fan blade turning.

Running.

Parachute filling.

Running.

Jumping.

The wind caught her and pulled her backwards into the air. The castle shrank below her feet. Her seat rocked back and forth at the wind's mercy. Taking her hand off the throttle, she reached up with both hands and grabbed the loops used to steer. Pain enflamed her left hand as she pulled down, causing the already broken bones to smash together.

Since she was going backwards, the paramotor banked right. After she had turned a bit, she pulled down with the right strap to even herself out. The wind stopped. She slid her hand out of the loop and back on the throttle, pushing the button to try and regain control of her aircraft back from the storm.

It worked.

The paramotor flew forward.

She pulled both loops and brought the paramotor closer to the ground to avoid any particularly powerful winds. She flew back over her house and said, "I'm coming, Mom," before banking hard to the left.

The next task would be equally difficult. The river flowed from the northeast down from the mountains to the north of Zero City, then banked south all the way down to the concrete river toward the border her mother told her to never cross.

"What would Hobbes say right now if I asked the odds of how far the river had carried mom?" she thought to herself. She figured the Flaggers started back up north where they dumped her and were working their way south. So, there was no reason to go back up there. If she went to the middle of the river to the west and made her way north, mom could have already floated past, and she would miss her.

She decided to start in the southwest corner where the two rivers met and work her way north. She set a course and flew low, just above the tree line, toward the river.

The forest around the watch tower swelled up and down like an emerald sea. Sparrow never ventured south of the watch tower because it was all forest. Her mother told her it was part of a national park once, but that it was one of the first wave of parks that were decommissioned in the mid-twenty-first century. From above, Sparrow could see old roads, nearly overgrown, cutting through the trees.

After a few minutes of gliding through the air, the ridge where the trees ended became visible. The rain was still falling, and she was completely soaked, but she knew the edge of the forest meant she was close to the small highway. Which meant she was getting closer to the river.

When the trees ended, she swooped down even lower to avoid the worst of the storm. She flew over the small highway that connected to the concrete river to the south and led to Zero City to the north. The road was empty. The cracks were filled with just as much plant life as she had seen farther north when she had walked that same road the day before with Rox, Teka, and Palo.

She had forgotten about them. She thought about where they might have headed when they left the subway. "Maybe they were on their way to get the paramotor," she thought. She remembered how much Palo had asked about it. Could she have beaten them back, though?

They had the disadvantage of not knowing where they were going, and they would have had to hike west around the lake.

"Maybe they went back to FerVR and tried to connect to The Stream again?" That seemed unlikely to Sparrow, considering how dangerous it was. They did seem desperate to get back into The Stream, though, which meant they would probably do anything.

"Rox would try to convince them to come back for me," she thought. This also seemed unlikely given the dangerous circumstances. She figured they assumed she was dead.

As Sparrow thought about these things, she soared near rolling fields of dead wheat, swaying back and forth in the wind just below her feet. Distracted by her thoughts, she pulled up just in time to narrowly miss colliding with a two-story red barn. A few more barns passed by, dotting the landscape all the way to the river.

The grey river that was the highway sat in eerie silence to her left. This was the farthest south she was allowed to go. Concrete blocks stacked on top of each other to form bridges. Dull grey roads slick with rainwater sat unused.

She could hear it before she could see it. The rain falling made a pattering noise, but the rushing water of the Great River made a constant whooshing sound. She painfully pulled both cords and rose higher into the air. Just ahead of her she could see the silver snake slithering as it cut through the land. It flowed under the concrete and metal bridge where the concrete river met the Great River. She banked around and lined herself up with the flowing water. She lowered her paramotor and began the search.

White foam bubbled up over the rapids near the bridge. She hoped her mother had not made it this far. There was no way anyone could survive those kinds of rapids. The water grew calmer as she kept flying north. The extended rainfall threatened to push the river up over the banks. And still the only things Sparrow saw were logs jammed and rocks rising out of the flow. No sign of her mother. No sign of life anywhere.

The river forked off into creeks and abandoned irrigation canals into farmers' fields from days gone by. The fields turned into rolling hills, and the rolling hills turned back into forest. All evidence of life was gone.

The river grew wider as Sparrow flew farther north. As it wound back and forth, Sparrow hovered over it, keeping her eyes on the flowing water.

After surveying the river for about ten minutes, she spotted a large structure on the opposite side of the river, amidst the trees. Once she flew a little closer, she could tell it was a large house. She guessed the mansion was the only structure in a five-mile radius. It had a large brick driveway leading up to the front door. The exterior was solid brick as well, but all the windows had thick metal bars across them. Solar panels covered the roof. She turned her head to get a better view when, suddenly, she heard a loud crack.

The same loud crack she heard the last time she saw Hobbes.

THIRTEEN

Sparrow looked up and saw a bullet hole in here parachute.

Without looking for the perpetrators, she pulled both loops down to lower herself below the tree line. Her feet were nearly skimming the water. She assumed it was the Flaggers, which meant they had not found her mother either.

She was trying to decide if she should turn around and look farther down the river, past the concrete river, when she saw something wrapped in a red cloth about a hundred feet ahead, stuck against a large fallen tree on the east side of the bank.

The trees grew right up to the edge of the river, making it impossible for her to land. So, she did the only thing she could. She flew toward the red wrapped thing, descending closer to the river, to the ground. In a snap she jerked forward and swung like a pendulum. She had crashed into a tree.

On purpose.

The parachute was stuck in some of the lower branches, and she swung back and forth before coming to a stop, suspended about ten feet off the ground. Sparrow hurriedly gathered herself, pulled the bo staff from the paramotor, then unbuckled her harness. She was able to slide out of the seat, holding on only with her right hand.

She let go.

She tried to do a barrel roll to ease the landing but ended up hitting with a solid thud in the cold mud. She was not concerned with any of her physical ailments. There was only one thing on her mind.

She ran up to the red cloth, splashing in the shallow water. The trees provided partial cover from the rain. This was it.

The moment she constantly questioned Hobbes about the probability.

The moment the family helped her reach.

The moment Trax encouraged her to find closure.

Tears filled her eyes as she reached down to the crimson cloth. She grabbed the wet wrap with her cold hand and began to pull the cloth away.

She gasped.

"How?"

After that first thought, her mind was filled with a barrage of hypotheticals.

Sparrow was standing in the shallow bank of the river when a voice called out behind her.

"Sparrow!"

She turned and pulled her bo staff out of instinct, thinking it to be one of the Flaggers. A chill washed down her spine. She was surprised to find her friend. Rox stood at the edge of the forest, with her mom and dad behind her. Rox, seeming to read Sparrow's mind, went on.

"We saw you flying over the river. Then we heard the gunshot and watched you go down. Did they get you?" she asked.

"Oh, no."

"But you crashed? Your hand?" Rox said, pointing to the paramotor in the tree.

"On purpose," Sparrow replied. "I thought this was my mom, but she's gone. She's not here. I lost her again. I lost her." Sparrow started crying again.

Teka emerged from behind the trees.

"Sparrow, I'm sorry we left you. And I'm sorry we lied to you. But your mom is okay. She escaped"

"How? Where is she?"

"We'll answer your questions, but we need to get out of here first. The Flaggers are close." Teka turned to her husband standing in the woods. "Palo, take us to the house."

He emerged from the woods with his head on a swivel surveying his surroundings like a scared kitten. Then he ran into the river.

Teka followed him.

"Stay with me," Rox said. She grabbed Sparrow's right hand and led her into the river. Then Rox grabbed her mother's hand, and her mother grabbed Palo's. They walked slowly across the river, crouching so their heads were just above the waterline. The riverbed was surprisingly smooth. They were able to cross in just a few minutes. Once on the other side, Palo sprinted south.

"Where are we going?" Sparrow asked between deep breaths, her mind reeling from the news of her mother.

"Our house," Rox replied.

"There are no houses around here for miles."

"Yeah, it's right there." Rox pointed to the mansion Sparrow had spotted earlier. They were only a few hundred yards away.

Palo led them away from the river and into the woods. There were no trails, but by the time the three family members cut through the brush, it was not so bad for Sparrow. While she pushed some bushes aside, she wondered how her mother had escaped and what Teka meant when she said she was sorry she lied to Sparrow.

Sparrow tried to replay all their conversations back to try and find the lie. She did not get very far before she walked into a clearing and was right next to the house. Palo led them around the brick walls and the barred windows to the front of the house.

They cut through dead shrubbery, over a fountain filling with rainwater, and, finally, came to a large, wooden door with no windows. Teka walked ahead of Palo, who was bent over with his hands on his knees, panting for air. She lifted a leather strap from around her neck.

It was a key.

She slotted it into a small keyhole, turned it, and pulled the door open. "Hurry," she said in a whisper, and the four of them ran inside. Teka closed the door, locked the deadbolt, and placed a wooden beam across the door. "That should do it," she said, satisfied.

"Where's Mom?" Sparrow demanded before Teka had even taken her hands off the beam. The four of them stood in a dark entryway, where a large chandelier dangled from the vaulted ceiling. A staircase led up to the second floor. The tan tile floor pooled with river water dripping from their clothes.

"When we left that subway, we got out of Zero City as fast as we could," Teka replied. She started walking further into the house, under the stairs and through a hallway. The other three followed. "We didn't know what else to do, so we figured we'd come back home to try to come up with another plan."

"The only problem was, we didn't know how to get home," Palo interjected. "We thought we would just go west until we hit the river and then follow it down to our house."

Teka opened a small door and looked inside. After a few seconds, she shook her head then closed it. She walked a bit further down the hallway and opened another door. This time she pulled out a towel and handed it to Sparrow. Then she handed towels to Rox and Palo before taking one for herself.

"We made it to the river and started walking down along the bank near that little town where we first saw you, Hornbill Ranch?" Teka said.

"Hornbeak Village," Sparrow said.

"Yeah, that one," Rox replied. "We heard a few people shouting up ahead." Rox looked at her mom, who was draping the towel around her daughter's shoulders.

"Of course, we thought it was the Flaggers at first, so we hid." She paused while she dried her hair with her own towel. "Then we got a good look at them and realized they were wearing nice suits."

"The people from the west?" Sparrow asked.

"From Ravenden," Teka confirmed. "And they were dragging something out of the river."

"Mom," Sparrow whispered.

"Yes."

"Was she—" Sparrow started to say. "Did she look—."

"She was moving," Rox replied. "She looked kind of beat up, but she was definitely moving a little."

Sparrow started weeping.

She buried her face in the towel.

"We would have gone after her," Rox continued, "but then we heard the sound of a motor and realized it was you flying up the river in the distance."

"We heard the shot and saw you go down," Teka said, her voice trembling. The glimpse of compassion made Sparrow look up from her towel. Tears filled Teka's eyes. She wiped them with a towel. "I thought they got you."

"You left me in the subway," Sparrow replied. "What do you care if they shot me?"

Teka tried to find words, but nothing came out. She walked farther down the hallway into a room. Sparrow followed. Rox and Palo followed behind her.

The room opened wide and tall and had a few leather couches, a piano, a small table; all covered with a heavy coat of dust. An empty fireplace was built into the wall, and above it a single cedar plank of wood was embedded in the wall. Picture frames were aligned on the mantle. Teka walked toward them.

She reached up and grabbed a frame and wiped off the dust with her damp shirt.

"This is why I care," Teka said, "and it's why I'm sorry."

She walked back over to Sparrow and handed her the frame.

Sparrow looked at the picture but couldn't make sense of it. There were three women and a child standing with a large red ribbon across them. One woman had shoulder length brown hair and a thin, wiry frame. She was holding a large pair of scissors.

"Is this you?" Sparrow asked.

"Yes," Teka replied, wiping her eyes.

Sparrow froze when she looked at another smiling woman in the picture. She had her hands on the shoulders of a young girl, who Sparrow guessed to be four or five years old. The woman was completely bald.

"Mom," Sparrow said.

"That's right," Teka replied. Rox and Palo looked just as confused as Sparrow.

"Then that's—"

"You, Sparrow, when you were a little girl."

"You knew my mom?" Sparrow asked.

"Very well," Teka replied.

"But, how? I don't remember you at all."

"This is the lie I'm sorry for," Teka replied. "Remember how I said I worked with your mom at FerVR?"

Sparrow nodded, unable to take her eyes from the picture.

"That was true," Teka replied, "but not honest. We worked together because we started the company together."

Sparrow's legs trembled at this revelation. She sat down on the couch before her legs gave out completely.

"No," Sparrow replied. "She never mentioned that. She would have told me."

"We had a falling out. There was an accident, Sparrow," Teka continued. She sat on the couch opposite of Sparrow. Palo sat next to his wife and Rox sat next to Sparrow. "We were working on a new headset that harnessed the user's brainwaves to increase immersion. I let you try a prototype before it had been completely approved."

"My scar," Sparrow tucked her hand under her leather helmet and ran her fingers over the raised scar tissue above her left ear.

"Yes." Teka looked at the ground. "The voltage was too high, and you passed out. You were in a coma for months. Once you woke up, you had lost all your anecdotal memory, including most of the experiences you had before the accident. Your mother and I were already not speaking because of company direction, but after that accident, she sold all her shares and left. I never heard from her again and didn't know where you both disappeared to until the other day, eleven years later, when you approached us in the woods."

"This is so much," Sparrow said. She ran her finger over the image of her mother.

"That's not all," Teka continued. Sparrow looked up. "Your mother, Trudy Hoodia, is my little sister."

Sparrow stood up at the revelation.

"You're lying!" Sparrow screamed. "She would have told me if she had a sister."

"She hated me for what I did to you. I hated myself for it." Teka stood up and went into another room. She came back a minute later with a piece of paper in her hand. She handed it to Sparrow and closed her eyes. "I'm sorry I didn't tell you sooner."

The paper had a picture of three young women on it, under a headline that read

SISTERS CREATE NEW EDEN, VR PARADISE.

"Why didn't you tell us, Mom?" Rox asked. "We left her to die up there in Zero City."

"I was trying to keep you safe," Teka said to her daughter. "I'm obviously a pretty lousy aunt and mother."

No one said anything for a few minutes.

Sparrow's mind was slowing down after having processed all this new information and trying to understand the implications. She was about to speak when the front door shuddered.

Shouts rose above the shaking of the wood door. "We know you're in there! We just want the bald one!"

"Flaggers," Sparrow whispered.

"Come on, Cueball. We won't hurt you," yelled another. "Come out! Come out!"

The yelling from the three or four Flaggers behind the door continued.

"That door will hold," Teka replied. "But we better get downstairs just in case. Rox?"

Rox jumped up from the couch and motioned for Sparrow to follow her. They went down another hallway near the fireplace and Rox opened a door. "Watch your step," she said as she led Sparrow down a stone staircase.

At the bottom of the stairs was a large rectangle vault door. She pushed it open. The room was mostly dark, the only light came in from the windows high on the wall. Under the windowed wall was a large bookcase filled with random pieces of technology. A circular rug filled the room. Sitting on the rug were what looked like three tombs in a row. Rox must have caught Sparrow staring.

"Those are the immersion tanks," Rox answered a question that hadn't been asked.

"So, that's where you live."

"For as long as I can remember," Rox replied.

"What's all of this," Sparrow said, turning her attention to the wall of electronics.

"Spare parts, mostly," Rox replied. "I think. Mom does all the little repairs, so I don't really know."

Sparrow walked near the shelf. In the faint light she saw wads of cords and wires. Power adapters and motherboards and screws and small fans. Little screens and bigger screens.

On the bottom shelf she found a round, metal ball about the size of a baseball. She lifted it from the dust and wiped it off. At the same time, Teka and Palo came through the vault door holding clothes and a bag. Palo closed the door and sealed it. Teka came over to Sparrow.

"Look familiar?" she said.

"Hobbes?" Sparrow asked.

"Oh no," Teka laughed. "That little thing was your mom's side project. One of a kind. A few years after she left, we sold these to the public. Watzon, we called it. People went crazy for them." She paused, thinking about the past. "Then, a little over a year later, the VR-evolution hit, and no one cared at all about them, as it usually goes. Hobbes was something like a prototype. I think we used some of the features, but we added some of our own as well."

Sparrow turned the metal ball over in her hand. She started to put it back on the shelf.

"Why don't you hold onto it for me," Teka said. "I don't need it anymore. I could never really get it to work anyway. Give it some sunlight and it should kick back on."

"Okay," Sparrow said. She walked over to the corner of the room where the light was hitting the floor and set down the metal ball. "There you go, Watzon."

"Did the Flaggers go away?" Rox asked.

"They were still pounding on the door when we came down here," Teka replied. "I bet they'll give up soon. Sparrow, let's get that hand cleaned up."

"We brought the last of our rations," Palo added, "and some dry clothes."

Teka grabbed a first aid kit from the bag and walked over to Sparrow. She sat down and motioned for her to sit down too. She did. Rox and Palo went to opposite dim corners and changed into dry clothes.

"I really am sorry, Sparrow," Teka said as she began to unwrap the shirt from Sparrow's wounded hand.

"Why did you hate each other?" Sparrow asked.

"What do you mean?"

"You said before the accident you both already hated each other because of company things. What does that mean?"

The broken hand was exposed. The skin was blue and purple around the crimson wound. Teka poured something on the wound that made it sting. Sparrow clinched her teeth.

"Your mother wanted to use virtual reality to enhance the way we interact with natural world. She wanted to use it to help people appreciate nature more. Easily identifying plants and birds, seeing how a specific piece of land has changed over the centuries, or will change. Planning a garden or homestead and seeing what it would look like once complete. Things like that."

"And you?"

"I wanted to push the limits and build new worlds that had previously only existed in dreams. That seemed to be what the general public wanted too.

"Few people wanted her mobile headsets for augmented exploration. She dreamed of being able to walk through a forest wearing glasses that identified and magnified birds high in treetops. More people wanted the tanks and full immersion. She thought we were pushing her out. This is going to hurt."

Teka grabbed Sparrow's hand and began taping

around the wrist and then up around her fingers and around her palm. Sparrow screamed. Rox came over and sat by her, now in a clean grey jumpsuit. Palo came over and stood, leaning against one of the tanks.

"You should probably eat," Rox said.

"We should all eat," Teka replied.

"We don't have that much food," Palo said. "We can't stay down here long. We already tried that. What's the plan?"

Sparrow stood and walked over to the wall where the windows were. She tested the shelves to see if they would hold her. They did. She climbed up and looked out the window. The storm had passed, and the sun was breaking through the clouds. It painted the mountains in a wonderful light.

"I don't know," Teka replied. "We'll figure it—"

"West." Sparrow interrupted. "We're going west. To Ravenden." She jumped down and stood on the opposite side of the room with the light shining behind her. "We're going to find my mom."

FOURTEEN

"Are you ready?" Sparrow called down to Rox. The rot-stricken floor of the barn creaked as Sparrow walked toward the ladder. Between the slits in the floor, she could see Rox putting something into a backpack on the ground level.

"Ready when you are," Rox called back. Sparrow descended the ladder, her good hand on the rungs and her broken hand tucked at her side. As she made her way to the dusty ground, Rox was pulling on a backpack.

"We've got to track down my mom," Sparrow said.

"We will," Rox replied. "My parents are trying to intercept any radio signals right now."

"I know," Sparrow replied. "We need to go track her down. Like, actually leave."

"She's still alive," Rox said, ignoring the pointedness of Sparrow's previous statement. "The suits from the west aren't going to hurt her. They rescued her after all."

"We shouldn't have stayed the night in your house," Sparrow replied.

"Those Flaggers were everywhere," Rox reminded her, "and we needed supplies."

"We have to leave today," Sparrow countered. She grabbed the handle of a blood-rust colored wagon and started rolling it away from Rox.

"And we will," Rox replied. She put her hand on her cousin's shoulder as they walked toward the giant, paint-chipped barn door. "I found something you might like." Rox reached into her pocket. In her extended open hand was a flattened gold sphere with a little arch on one side and a button on the other. A bird in mid-flight was etched into the side. Dirt filled the crevices of the engraving. A thin rope had been thread through the arch.

"Thanks," Sparrow said, taking the gift. "What is it?"

"I don't know," Rox replied. "I found it on one of the shelves in the house. The bird made me think of you. Push that little button on the top."

Sparrow pressed the top and the gold casing split to reveal numbers and black arrows.

"I think people used to tell time with these," Sparrow said.

"How?"

"I have no idea," Sparrow replied. She lifted the necklace over her head. The pocket watch rested just under her collar bone. "Thank you, Rox."

"You're welcome," Rox replied. "Now, let's get out of here and go find your mom." Rox ran over to the barn door to pull it open. It didn't budge. She dug her heels into the dirt, but still nothing. Sparrow smiled and used her good hand to help her friend and the door rolled open on its tracks, just enough for them to fit the wagon through.

The sun was low behind the mountain range to the east. Sparrow and Rox had left before the sunrise to venture south to the abandoned farmhouse. The cold air bit their noses as they emerged from the barn. Rox pulled on the knit hat she had brought from her house. Sparrow still wore her leather football helmet. Their breath escaped in a ghostly white fog.

"I didn't know it got this cold outside of The Stream," Rox said, crossing her arms over her chest to try to stay warm.

"It's almost spring," Sparrow said with a laugh. "You're lucky it's not January."

"What happens in January?"

"You have to know about snow," Sparrow replied.

"It snows here?" Rox asked. Her eyes lit up and a smile revealed her teeth. "That's amazing."

"What do you think that white stuff is?" Sparrow pointed to snow-capped mountain range.

"That's snow, too?" Rox replied. "I've been to Alaska in The Stream, of course, for school or to see the sea monsters or something. I didn't know that happened here."

"I don't think it's like Alaska, but we get some."

"Have you ever made a snowman?" Rox asked.

"Of course," Sparrow replied.

"That's so cool."

"If you stick around after we save my mom, we can build one next winter."

"I'd like that," Rox replied.

They walked north, away from the barn, and started the journey back to Rox's mansion where they had hunkered down the night before. They were coming up on a two story, square house with busted windows and a wraparound porch that had fallen in on itself.

"Find anything else in there?" Sparrow asked.

"A couple cans of something. Artichoke hearts?"

"Yuck," Sparrow replied.

"You've had them?"

"They're common these days. Which means people must not have liked them too much if we keep finding them everywhere."

"I found some more matches."

"That's great."

"And these gloves." Rox held out her hands and turned them over a few times.

"Those look warm."

"They are," Rox replied. "I got this to add to my collection of pre-VR stuff, so I don't think we can use it, but it's an old piece of paper with Zero City drawn on it."

"Let me see that," Sparrow said. Rox unfolded the paper and handed it to Sparrow, who set it on the ground. She knelt and began pointing to different spots on the paper.

"This is a map, Rox," she said. "It's old, but this is about where my house is. Here are the mountains. And here's the road we traveled on to get to Zero City."

"My house must be around here or something, right?" Rox asked, as she pointed to a spot west of the river.

"I think that's right. And we're here somewhere," Sparrow said, pointing to the bottom left-hand corner of the map. "Ravenden must be pretty far west. It's not on here."

"Do you think the people who saved your mom swam across the river?"

"They couldn't have. It's too fast up by the city." Sparrow said.

"But the river comes down from the mountains and circles Zero City. They had to cross it somehow." Sparrow looked down at the map and put her finger on the river near Rox's mansion. Then she moved North, looking for any thin spots where her mother's captors might have crossed. The blue line got wider as she moved her finger north. She followed the river as it curved to the east, toward the mountains, until she was above Zero City. She kept going, and then she saw it.

"Look," Sparrow said, louder than necessary. "A bridge!"

"At the base of the mountains," Rox replied. "They must have crossed there."

"That's where we'll cross, too," Sparrow said. She began to fold up the map.

"But we're already across the river," Rox replied.

"We've got one more stop to make," Sparrow said. "This is a great find, Rox."

"Oh, okay. Well, it was an accident," Rox replied. "I just thought it looked cool."

"I've got more stuff like this back at the castle," Sparrow said.

"Like what?" Rox asked, her eyes widening.

"Some binoculars and a yo-yo."

"I'd like to see those," Rox replied.

"You will."

Rox smiled.

They walked along a hard, nearly frozen dirt path. The wagon bounced at every rock and crevice. With every bounce of the wagon, they left the farmland behind. After the wagon clanked for a few minutes, Rox spoke up.

"That's loud."

"I think one of the wheels is loose. Just needs to be tightened up."

"Do we need it?"

"Just for carrying things easier."

"We can carry our own stuff," Rox replied. "And it's kind of annoying."

"It won't be annoying when I fix the wheel," Sparrow laughed. "And we need to pick something up at the train yard on our way out of town."

"That's why we need the bridge," Rox replied. "What is it?"

"Not what," Sparrow replied. "Who."

"What?" Rox repeated, with excitement in her voice.

"When I left the subway, I thought my mom was dead. Hobbes had been destroyed. And I killed..." Sparrow trailed off. She had not had time to process the events over the past day. Rox was silent. "I wanted to die," Sparrow continued. "I ran and ran and ran until I came to the train yard. I opened one of the old train cars and got inside, with no plan to leave. But there was already someone inside."

"Who?" Rox asked, turning toward Sparrow.

"His name is Trax."

"What was he doing?"

"His legs are all beat up. Some dogs attacked him."

"That's what the wagon is for," Rox replied, "because he can't walk."

"Yeah," Sparrow replied. "He's got family in Ravenden. We're going to take him up there."

"I don't think my mom will like that," Rox said.

"None of us have been to Ravenden. Trax has. He'll lead us there."

"She still won't like it."

"She doesn't have to come," Sparrow snapped back. An awkward silence hung in the air. The wagon bumped up and down behind them. The farm was out of sight now, and the river rushed past to their left. The mansion was a speck on the horizon ahead of them.

After a few minutes, Sparrow spoke. "I'm sorry."

"I didn't mean to upset you."

"You didn't," Sparrow replied. "It's just been a lot these last few days."

"Of course."

"I don't yell often."

"It's okay," Rox said.

"You're a good friend."

"You're my only friend," Rox replied. "My only real not-in-The-Stream friend at least."

"You're my only not-a-robot-companion friend."

They both laughed.

"Speaking of robot friends," Rox said. "Did you get Watzon to work?"

Sparrow stopped the wagon and reached into her backpack. She pulled out a small, jet-black metal sphere and handed it to Rox.

"Nope. Nothing," she replied.

"Wait! Look!" Rox yelled. She turned the ball over and showed Sparrow.

"What?"

"A light blinked. Did you see it?"

"No," Sparrow replied. "Are you sure? It could have been a reflection from the sun."

"Oh," Rox said, deflated. "I thought I saw a light blink."

"Maybe you did," Sparrow said. "I'll keep trying to get it to turn on."

"Okay," Rox said, handing the ball back to Sparrow.

"Thanks," Sparrow said. "Let's hurry back."

"Why?" Rox asked. "It's a beautiful day."

"We're leaving today."

"Do we have everything?" Palo asked. Teka pulled a key out of the front door. She tested the lock. The door did not budge.

"Yes, Palo," Teka replied without looking at her husband. "We both double checked."

"It's a long trip, okay?" he said.

"I know this, dear," she replied. "The girls found some food at the farm. I've packed up the rest of the stuff we had here. There's nothing left to take."

"Okay," Palo replied.

"Hope you like artichoke hearts," Rox joked.

Palo grimaced. Teka and Sparrow laughed in unison. The joyous moment was short-lived as they looked at each other right away and stopped. Teka addressed the tension.

"We're a family and families tell the truth. I'm sorry for not telling you the truth, Sparrow."

Sparrow locked eyes with her aunt, but only one word came out. "Okay."

"I understand," Teka replied. "I'll work at building your trust back."

"We should get going," Sparrow replied. She picked up the wagon handle and started down the stone driveway. They walked in silence. The chilly April wind moved through the trees. A few birds sang in the distance. The sun hung in the morning sky. The sound of the river trickling by grew louder as they approached.

"Why are we crossing the river?" Teka asked. "It flows from the mountains. It's too violent to cross up there."

"And we're already on the other side," Palo added.

Rox looked at Sparrow.

"We need to get something at the train yard," Sparrow said.

"That's by Zero City," Palo exclaimed. "I'm not going back up there."

"I made a promise," Sparrow said.

"A Flagger?" Teka asked, before Palo could get another word in.

Sparrow told Teka and Palo about Trax, and how she promised to reunite him with his family in Ravenden.

"And he's been there before. He can be our guide," Sparrow added.

Teka had a far off look on her face. Sparrow figured her aunt was thinking this through. Palo waited for Teka's response. A shadow danced on the ground as a hawk flew overhead.

"Of course, Sparrow," Teka said. Palo turned a sharp glance toward his wife. She did not acknowledge him. "Guess we better figure out how to get this wagon across the river, yeah?"

"Um, yeah," Sparrow replied, shocked at Teka's eagerness.

"I bet you and dad could hold it above your heads while we walk across," Rox suggested. "We can take the supplies out so it's not too heavy. Can you carry some stuff, Sparrow? With your hand and all?"

"I can manage," Sparrow replied.

"Let's do it," Teka said with enthusiasm.

Sparrow was skeptical of Teka's transformation, but she was glad for the help. She helped Rox unpack the wagon. They placed a sack of clothes, cans and pouches of food, and their backpacks on the ground.

"You take the back," Teka said to her husband. "Rox, you go behind your father. Sparrow, you lead us across."

A moment later, the liquid ice flowed over the top of Sparrow's boots, trickling between her toes. She held a bag with clothes, food, and Watzon over her head with her good hand. Her bandaged broken hand bobbed above the water.

"Should. Have. Taken. Boots. Off," Sparrow chattered as the water reached her waist. The family laughed through chattering teeth. Sparrow smiled. A warmth filled her chest.

The hardest part of crossing the river was the frigid cold. It flowed slow enough that there was no danger of being washed downstream. Once they made it to the other side, the family set the supplies down and huddled together.

"We need to change into warm clothes," Teka said.

"We need to make a fire," Palo added.

"There's no time for that," Sparrow replied. "We're already behind."

"We'll freeze out here."

"Palo, dear, calm down," Teka said. "We're not thinking straight. Let's change into warm clothes and then we'll figure it out."

With that, the family broke from the huddle and hurried toward their bags of clothes. Sparrow quickly discarded the soaked brown sweater, now nearly black with water, and pulled a large parka over her head. She pulled off the wet boots and socks and replaced them with Christmas-red long underwear.

As she laid her wet clothes on the ground, she heard a crash in the metal wagon next to her. A branch had fallen, and she heard a scurry in the tree above her. A squirrel retreated through the branches. She looked back at the branch in the wagon and got an idea.

"What if we made a fire and kept walking," she said as the newly outfitted group reconvened around the wagon.

"I'm listening," Palo replied.

"We need to stay warm, and dry our stuff, but we need to keep moving," Sparrow continued. "What if we made a fire in the wagon and pulled it with us?"

The family was silent for a moment as they mulled it over. Teka started to speak a few times, trying to find a fault in the plan, but no words came out.

"I love it," Rox said.

"We'll have to carry our supplies," Teka replied. "But we were doing that, anyway." Teka paused to give her face a moment to light up. "Let's go gather some wood."

With the four of them working together, it didn't take long to gather enough wood for their mobile fire. They piled all the wood next to the wagon and waited for Sparrow to work her magic.

"You're up," Palo said.

"Oh, right," Sparrow replied. She thought back to the fire she had created days ago under Hobbes' guidance. She imitated the same process, only this time on a smaller scale. She built the base of the fire in the back end of the wagon, planning to use the front half to dry clothes.

"Can wagons carry fire?" Rox asked as Sparrow finished up the structure.

"I don't know," Sparrow replied. "This isn't a thing that people do," she laughed. "It's metal, though. Seems sturdy. I think it will hold. Anyone have matches?"

Teka reached into her bag and handed Sparrow a box of matches. Sparrow gathered some leaves and twigs and placed them in the kindling spot of her structure. She held her breath and struck the match. A few moments later, after blowing into the small flame, the twigs were starting to catch. They had a fire on wheels.

"We can take turns putting our wet clothes on this

side," Sparrow said, pointing toward the empty front half of the wagon. "Should dry them pretty quick."

"Are we ready to go?" Teka asked, grabbing the handle.

Everyone nodded in unison, slung their bags over their shoulders, and took off barefoot up the bank of the river. Sparrow and Rox placed their shoes near the fire. Palo carried all the wet clothes in his pack. Everyone else walked next to the rolling flames, warming their hands and faces.

They decided to risk traveling the main road. Speed was their chief concern, so they set out, traveling north, keeping an eye out for Flaggers. The rolling fire cracked and popped with each bump of the road. Sparrow saw a squirrel jumping from tree to tree parallel to the road. It cocked its head sideways in what Sparrow interpreted as confusion when it looked at the rolling fire. A moment later, it soared to another branch and was swallowed by the forest.

The afternoon was uneventful, which was exactly what Sparrow needed. Zero City's ghostly skyline was now visible on the horizon. The family stopped for a break and Teka helped her niece change the bandages. Palo sprawled out like a pancake on the road. Rox went to gather more wood for the dying fire.

"Feel any better?" Teka asked.

"It hurts more now than when that bear crushed it," Sparrow replied.

"Your adrenaline has worn off," her aunt replied. "Good news is that means your brain doesn't think you're in danger. Bad news is now the pain is going to hurt like hell."

"Thanks," Sparrow replied.

Rox came back to the group with an armload of sticks just as Teka removed the last bandage from Sparrow's hand. Deep red streaks of dried blood crisscrossed around and through the exposed flesh.

Rox puked on her bare feet.

"It's that bad, huh?" Sparrow asked.

"Sorry," Rox said, wiping her mouth.

"It's worse than I thought," Teka replied. "It doesn't look infected, but I don't think I can set these bones. There's so many and they're all shattered."

"Has the bleeding stopped?" Sparrow asked.

"Looks like it," Teka replied.

"Okay, let's wrap it up and keep going. We need to get to the rail yard before it gets dark."

Five minutes later, they were walking north on the main road toward the rail yard.

Their pace as a family was much faster than their pace, just days before, as strangers. They put one foot in front of the other with confidence. The familiar path helped them move at a quicker pace. Yet, they were just outside of Zero City when the sun set behind them.

"Better put that fire out," Teka said. "Flaggers will be able to see it from the city."

"Need to get our clothes back on," Palo added. "Getting cold."

They paused, dumped the fire in some dirt, and stomped it out. They fumbled around in the dark as they put on their damp clothes. Teka spoke as she pulled a sweater over her head.

"Following you, Sparrow. Should we camp here for the night, or are the trains close?"

"We can keep going," Sparrow replied.

The family nodded in the dim light and Sparrow took off east, around Zero City.

Less than an hour later, the grass turned into patchy gravel and sleeping metal train cars reflected the moonlight ahead of them.

They walked around the maze of train cars for a few minutes before Palo spoke, "Which one is it?"

"Just over here," Sparrow replied. "I think."

"You think?" Palo asked.

"Let's spread out," Rox said. Her mother looked at her. "Not too far, of course."

"Great idea," Sparrow replied. "His name is Trax. He's an old man."

"I'm sure there aren't many people out here," Teka replied.

The family dispersed. Sparrow crept along, trying to recognize Trax's train car amidst the identical cars, the gravel crunching with every step. Right away, she found one that looked familiar. She slid the door open a crack.

"Trax?" Sparrow whispered.

FIFTEEN

"What if that was the right train car, but I'm too late," she asked herself while walking to the next train car.

Sparrow's eyes flared at the grim realization. She ran back to the train car and pulled the door all the way open, so the moonlight could creep in. As she looked inside the car, she found small metal boxes overturned in a pile, but no sign of Trax.

She exhaled.

"He's alive. He must be," Sparrow thought as she walked to another car. Lost in her thoughts, she dropped her head. She saw small craters darkened by the moonlight. She realized they weren't craters at all, but footprints. Specifically, her footprints from when she left Trax and sprinted to the castle the day before.

She followed them until they stopped in front of a matte grey train car.

She slid the door open and was met by a familiar

voice. "I'm not going to do you no harm. I'm a friend. Not going to hurt you."

"Trax!" Sparrow called out.

"Sparrow?" he replied. "I don't believe it. You came back."

"I said I would."

"Did you find your mom?"

"No, but she's still alive. Some people took her west. Heading for Ravenden. That's where we're heading, and I'd like for you to come with us."

"Oh, well I appreciate the offer. I'm afraid these legs haven't healed up at all, so I won't be going anywhere."

"I thought you might say that," Sparrow replied. "We've got a way to get you there. We need your help since you've been there before. We don't know the way."

"You going to carry me all that way?" Trax replied.

"Something like that."

THE SUNLIGHT CUT through a crack in the train car like a thin strip of gold. Sparrow woke first and slid the door halfway open, the light washed over the family, and Trax, all sleeping inside. The air bit colder than the morning before, sending a warning that winter was trying to hang on as long as it could.

"We need to get going," Sparrow said, her voice echoing off the metal walls. No one spoke, but they pulled themselves up from their slumber, and prepared for the day. Trax slid over to the opening of the train car and opened his arms wide.

"Who gets to do the honors?" Trax said, a laugh starting deep in his belly.

"We've got something better than that," Sparrow replied. She ducked under the train car.

"You got a horse under there?"

A second later, Sparrow pulled the wagon out from its hiding place under the belly of the train car. She parked it by the door. Trax looked down at it, then to the family.

"You're serious?" He said, not in a sarcastic tone, but with genuine sincerity. "You all are going to pull this mangled, old stranger the whole way?"

"You better get in before I start thinking about it too long," Sparrow laughed. Trax put one arm around Sparrow, and one around Palo, as he lowered himself, slowly, into the wagon. His legs sat crooked in front of him. In the sunlight, Sparrow could see his gaunt face, white like the top of the mountains.

"Comfortable?" Rox asked.

"Yes, ma'am," Trax replied. "Remind me your name again? Memory isn't as good as it used to be. Can't even remember last night when you all introduced yourselves."

"It's okay," Rox replied. "It's Roxana, but everyone calls me Rox."

"Rox, that's right. A good name that is, 'specially since it ends with an X."

"Ready to get going?" Sparrow asked him.

"I think so," Trax replied.

Sparrow picked up the handle again, with her good hand, and the wagon rolled forward.

They made a wide circle around the east side of Zero City, to avoid the Flaggers. It added some time to their trip, but they all agreed it was well worth the trouble. The sun had begun its ascent as they put the abandoned city behind them. The air was cool near the base of the mountains to their right. Sparrow kept adjusting her grip on the wagon.

"Need me to take a turn?" Teka asked.

"Oh, it's okay," Sparrow replied.

"If you get me two big sticks, I'll bet I can row myself like a boat," Trax replied.

"I just need to find a good hold," Sparrow replied.

"Sparrow," Teka said, now standing in front of her niece. "You have a broken hand, and you're half the size of that man. You've done enough. Take a break." Sparrow glanced from Palo, to Rox, to Trax, before tears filled her eyes. No words were spoken, but she handed the wagon grip over to Teka. "Rox, get Sparrow some water."

The wagon rolled away. Sparrow waited behind as Rox dug through her bag.

"I know it's in here somewhere," she said.

"It's okay," Sparrow replied. "I'm not that thirsty."

"You must be," Rox insisted. "You've been pulling that old man for a couple hours."

"It'd be a piece of cake if I had both hands."

"A piece of cake?" Rox asked. They both began walking.

"You don't know what, 'a piece of cake' is?"

"I mean, I know what cake is. People have rebuilt entire cities with cake in The Stream. Las Cakegas,

Bangcake, Tocakyo, stuff like that. I've never heard that saying, though."

"Tocakyo? Sounds like a waste of time," Sparrow replied. "Anyway, it just means it would be really easy. No sweat at all."

"Oh," Rox replied.

"Yeah," Sparrow replied, looking down at her broken hand.

"It'll heal," Rox said.

"Your mom didn't seem too sure."

"She's not a doctor. She doesn't know," Rox paused and looked at her parents up ahead. "She knows a lot, but she pretends to know a lot, too."

"It does feel better," Sparrow replied. "Whatever she did."

"You're on your way to being a two handed, flying, survivalist again." They both laughed a little.

"Tell me more about Las Cakegas," Sparrow said.

They walked for another hour or so, stopping occasionally for Teka to take a break before they heard water rushing down the mountain side. The bridge was just up ahead.

"That water looks cold," Palo said, cinching his jacket across his body.

"Looks like that old map was right," Teka said, allowing Trax to roll to a stop. "This bridge has been here a long time." The group surveyed the old bridge glazed with the late day sunlight. Wooden boards were cracked, others were missing entirely. Sparrow guessed the bridge was painted at some point, but now the wood was covered in green moss.

"It'll hold," Sparrow said.

"Should we pull the wagon across first?" Rox asked. "If it can hold the wagon, it could hold any of us."

"I think I just got called fat," Trax laughed.

"I didn't mean any—"

"I'm just pulling your cord," Trax replied. "Anyway, best to bring me across last, in case the bridge does fall through. Don't want you all to be stranded over here if I go for a swim."

"Trax," Sparrow said. "It'll hold."

"Of course, it will."

"You all go first," Sparrow said to her family. "I'll pull Trax after you all are safe on the other side."

"Are you sure?"

"We're losing daylight."

The family secured their belongings tightly to their backs before approaching the bridge. It was decided that Rox would go first, as the lightest and most likely to make it across. She hugged her mom and dad, burying her face in her mom's sleeve, before taking a deep breath and approaching the mouth of the bridge.

She put a foot onto the first board, applying her weight gradually. Once satisfied with its stability, she did the same with the next board. Then the next. Her speed increased as she reached the middle of the bridge. She placed her hands on the railing on both sides to help distribute the weight. She cleared the second half in a fraction of the time it took her to clear the first. She jumped over the last couple boards and landed safely on the opposite bank.

Teka went next. Palo followed close behind. They both crossed with no problem.

It was Sparrow's turn to pull Trax across.

"You don't have to do this," Trax said. "You could just drop me in that river, and I'll ride it down to the lake. That's not a bad way to go out. I'd get to see the lake, after all."

"I'm not leaving you here or putting you in the river or anything like that," Sparrow replied. "I'm taking you up to see your family."

"I can't tell if you're that dumb or that special," Trax replied.

"Here we go," Sparrow said.

She pulled the wagon onto the first board. The mist from melted snow covered her face and hand. She readjusted her grip on the handle and began to pull. The boards creaked and moaned beneath the weight.

"I can try to lighten the load by holding on to the handrails," Trax said. He extended both arms and lifted some of his weight from the wagon.

The bridge held.

She kept pulling her cargo, trying not to look down, but she couldn't resist. She needed to see where the boards were missing to navigate the wagon. She saw white foam and dark rocks in the empty spaces beneath her. Trax readjusted his grip on the rails as they moved forward.

They reached the middle of the bridge.

Sparrow kept going, eyes down to avoid a hole, when she heard a muted crack of damp wood, followed by a yell from Trax.

She spun her head around, expecting to see Trax falling into the river. But the wagon was still there. The wood beneath the wagon had not snapped. The wooden rail, where Trax was holding on, snapped clean off and now lay across his mauled legs.

A bright red filled his bandaged legs. He had impaled one of his wounded legs with the sharp edge of the splintered handrail when it broke.

Sparrow turned, wagon in hand, and sprinted toward dry ground.

The wagon bounced along the uneven boards as Sparrow sprinted to the opposite bank. She was sure Trax left the seat of the wagon a few times as they bounced onto the shore. The wagon held. The bridge held. They were safe on dry land.

Sparrow brought the wagon to a stop to tend to Trax. The flow of fresh blood on his bandages seemed to have stopped. Trax was laying back in the wagon with his eyes closed. Sparrow assumed the worst.

"Trax! No!" she yelled.

The injured man raised his eyelids casually, like someone had just woken him from a nap. A smirk stretched across his face.

"I'm still here," he said, his voice raspy.

"Your legs," Sparrow motioned. The family had joined, and now stood in a half circle around Trax.

"Did it to myself this time. Pulled the railing clear off and reopened some of the wounds," he said as he adjusted the bandages tenderly. "I think I'll be fine."

"I'm sorry, Trax," Sparrow replied.

"I wouldn't be here without you."

"I know, that's why I'm sorry."

"That ain't what I mean," he replied. "I mean, thank you. I'd have died, all on my own, in a train. At least I got friends now."

Sparrow didn't reply.

"I can take a look at it when we make camp tonight," Teka said, breaking the silence.

"We should find camp soon," Trax replied with a half laugh.

"He's right," Palo added. "Let's go."

"I'll take a turn on the wagon," Teka replied. She picked up the handle and led the way west.

"Thank you all," Trax said. "It's nice to be part of a family again."

No one replied, though they shared Trax's sentiment. They walked, up and down slow rolling hills, until the sun touched the horizon to their left. Trax had fallen asleep in the wagon. Palo walked with his wife. Sparrow and Rox followed a few paces behind the wagon. Sparrow could see her breath fog as it left her mouth.

"We need to start a fire," Sparrow called ahead. "Let's make camp here."

"Looks like as good a spot as any," Teka replied. "We'll go get some firewood. Sparrow, you stay with Trax."

The family left. Sparrow let the old man rest. She looked at the prairie land ahead of them, and then sat down against a tree and pulled the metal bot, Watzon, from her bag.

She turned it over and over, checking the ports. She found where she guessed the solar panels retracted from but was unable to pry them open. As she was trying, the family returned.

"Watzon's a shy bot," Rox called out as she set down an armful of sticks.

"I think if I can get these solar panels out, I can get it fully functioning." Sparrow said.

"That would be helpful right now," Teka replied.

"What can it do, again?" Sparrow asked.

"Well," Teka replied, "it can fly and spot enemies and all that stuff, like your other bot."

"Hobbes," Sparrow corrected her.

"Yes, like Hobbes," Teka said. "There are some other features, but the main one is that Watzon can connect to The Stream."

"Don't you have to be plugged in?" Sparrow asked.

"That's the best way, but no." Teka paused before continuing. "The Stream is all around us."

Sparrow was sure she had a visibly confused look on her face, which is probably what prompted her aunt to continue.

"The Stream can be accessed from anywhere, wirelessly. You just need a way to access it."

"That doesn't make sense."

"It's like this," Rox added, "what if you could take the door off your castle, and carry it anywhere, and anytime you opened it, you would be back in your castle. Your castle would be accessible from anywhere with your new magic door. The Stream is like that. We just don't have a door."

"A working door," Teka motioned to Watzon.

"Okay," Sparrow replied, only half understanding the

talk about magic doors. "I'll keep working on Watzon then."

"Could you help us start a fire first?" Palo asked.

Less than ten minutes later, the entire party sat circled around the small fire. The sun had set, and the nightly chill was all around them. They were bundled in many layers. If they moved an inch closer to the flames, their clothes would've caught fire.

Trax was still asleep in the wagon. Sparrow checked his breathing between stints working on Watzon. Teka had made some kind of artichoke heart soup that tasted like dirt, but, since she was starving, she ate it without complaint.

"Fire's dying," Palo said, breaking the peaceful post-dinner silence.

"Go get some more sticks, then," Teka replied. Palo shifted his eyes at his wife.

"I'll do it," Sparrow said. "Keep an eye on Trax?"

"Of course," Teka replied.

Sparrow rocked forward and rolled to her feet. A long, coat hung down below her knees. She took in one last wisp of the fire's warmth before turning her back on camp and heading into the surrounding woods. The moonlight broke through the sparsely leafed trees, guiding Sparrow's path.

She spent about fifteen minutes gathering larger logs she hoped would burn for a long time. She was able to use her good hand to tuck the small logs under the arm with the broken hand. Once her arms were full, she turned and headed back to camp.

Back to where she thought camp was.

She was still so used to having Hobbes help her move through the world, she had not been diligent about remembering the direction back to camp. She took a few deep breaths and headed toward, what she assumed was, her camp.

She stepped over logs and crunched leaves, and before she knew it, she could see the faint glow of orange between the trees. She breathed a sigh of relief and walked toward the light. As she grew nearer, she realized the fire was much larger than when she left.

"They must have gotten impatient and found their own firewood," she thought.

But, when she moved around a large tree, she saw three people sitting around the fire. Two sat comfortably, fully bundled up with hats and gloves, talking and eating something. The third had her hands bound and her head exposed.

Her bald head exposed.

It was Sparrow's mother.

The firewood crashed at Sparrow's feet. She sprinted toward her mother until her rational brain took over. These people from the west would easily capture her as well. She needed reinforcements.

"Hold on, Mom," she whispered. She turned and ran toward where she hoped her family was still enjoying their dying fire.

Her mind raced faster than her feet. Before she knew it, she saw the dying light of a fire ahead of her. Palo jumped when Sparrow burst from the woods.

"My mother!" she yelled. "Just ahead. Tied up. Let's go!" The short sentences were not due to the urgency she felt, rather, they were a necessity of speaking between gulps of air after sprinting through the woods.

"How?" Teka asked.

"What do you mean?" Sparrow replied, pulling her bag over her shoulder. "Let's go."

"They left long before us," Teka replied. "They should be days ahead of us."

"We have to go," Sparrow replied. "I'll pull Trax."

"How far is it?" Palo asked.

"Not far. Let's go."

"Leave the wagon here," Palo said. Sparrow froze at this idea. She hadn't considered leaving Trax here. It wasn't too far away; he would be fine. But, before Sparrow had time to decide to leave her friend, Teka spoke.

"I can do it," Teka said, eyeing her husband. "You lead the way. Rox, will you put this fire out?"

"Yes ma'am," Rox replied.

"I guess I'll grab the bags," Palo said.

Less than a minute later the fire was smoldering, the darkness surrounded them, and they followed Sparrow through the woods. Trax's wagon bounced over twigs and rocks, but he remained unconscious.

Sparrow's mind drifted to the upcoming confrontation. She hoped she would be able to talk the people from the west into letting her mother go. She played out the scenario where they refused. The one where Sparrow would be forced to pull out her bo staff and fight one handed. This thought made her broken hand tremble. She wondered if she would be able to fight again, to kill, if it meant rescuing her mother.

She wasn't sure.

She was sure of one thing, though. An orange glow from a fire flickered just ahead of them. As they drew closer, there was only one figure sitting around the fire. It was her mother, wrists and legs still bound.

"The people from the west are gone," Sparrow whispered.

"Why would they leave her alone," Rox replied at the same volume.

"I don't know," Sparrow replied with an edge in her voice. "We need to—"

A sting pierced the flesh on Sparrow's exposed neck. She went to swat the bug away, but she couldn't find her neck. Her arms waved miserably for a few moments before her open palm landed with a smack on her neck. She heard two thumps, like falling rocks, behind her. The bug on her neck was soft as she yanked it free. She took one look at it and noticed it wasn't a bug at all. It was a little feather with a point on the end.

"That's pretty," she thought, before passing out.

SIXTEEN

The sunlight coming in through the window woke Sparrow. The concrete was smooth and cold on the side of her face. Sparrow sat up and looked around the room. There were glass walls surrounding her on three sides, creating a small room. Outside of the room, white walls with long skinny windows filled the length of the building. The small room sat suspended in the air looking over the large room. Rows of coffin-shaped boxes, immersion tanks, lined the large room below her.

Inside the small room, a tall figure stood in the shadows, face obscured, by a door in the only wall not made of glass. A small bank of computer screens sat against the window overlooking the large room. Three familiar bodies lay on the concrete surrounding Sparrow, along with one she hadn't seen in weeks.

"Mother!" Sparrow yelled. She fell on the body passed out next to her. The body started to move.

"Sparrow?" her mother asked.

"I thought I'd lost you." Sparrow wrapped her arms around her mother's neck, ignoring the pain in her hand. "We waited in the tower, but then it was a couple weeks, and I know I'm not supposed to fly alone, but I had to come after you, so we went out and met these people and—"

"Sparrow," her mother said, propping herself up on her arm. "What happened to your hand?" Sparrow tucked her head into her mother's chest and wept. Before Sparrow could respond, her mother spoke again.

"Teka?"

Sparrow popped her head up and wiped her eyes. The three family members were waking up, surveying these new surroundings, just as Sparrow had done.

"They helped me get here," Sparrow said.

Silence followed as Sparrow's mother and Teka stared at each other. Rox and Palo moved to the glass wall overlooking the huge cathedral-like room full of tanks.

"I couldn't have found you without them," Sparrow continued.

"Trudy," Teka said. "Didn't think I'd see you again."

"I hoped I wouldn't," Trudy replied.

"That's the sister I remember. Still mad after all these years?"

"You almost killed my daughter."

"And she would have never found you if it wasn't for us," Teka replied, standing up. Trudy followed. "Said so herself."

"It's true," Sparrow added.

"Guess we're all square, then," Teka said.

"Hmmph," Trudy replied.

"Good enough for me," Teka said. "This is the famous Sanctum at Ravenden, I take it?"

"Nothing gets past the world's leading virtual immersion scientist," Trudy replied.

"Why does that Roark lady want you, Mom?" Sparrow asked.

"Not going to stay long enough to find out. Let's go, Sparrow." Trudy made her way to the door but froze as she noticed the figure in the shadows for the first time. "We're leaving."

"So soon?" the figure said. A woman's voice. "The reunion's just begun."

"Don't think she wants to spend time gossiping," Teka laughed. "She's never been the touchy-feely type."

"You've wasted your time putting this meeting together," Trudy said.

"After all these years, you haven't changed a bit. Focus so narrow, you only see the leaves," the woman's voice said.

"Ah, a fan of our work. Makes sense now why you brought us here," Trudy said.

"In a way, yes. I've been a fan since the day I was born," the woman in the shadows said. "And have been looking forward to this day nearly as long."

"Sulla," Trudy said. "We're leaving." She grabbed Sparrow's arm and made her way to the door. Just then, a short woman with black hair pulled into a tight bun, wearing black pants and a black jacket, holding a metal walking stick, stepped out from the shadows. A tall woman stood behind her, still in the shadows. Sparrow heard Teka gasp from behind her. Trudy froze.

"No one's leaving yet, big sister."

"What?" Sparrow said, her mouth staying open in disbelief.

"Just like the old Trudy, wishing we never existed, now acting like we don't," Sulla said resting both hands on her long, thin walking stick. "Am I right, Tek?"

"Why did you kidnap us?" Teka asked.

"You mean, save your life?" Sulla replied with raised eyebrows. She dismissed the security guard, who stepped back into the shadows.

"You wouldn't have survived much longer out there, out there in the real world. I've given you what you wanted all along. Come, let me show you around a bit."

Sulla turned and made her way toward the door. The female security guard stepped out of the shadows and circled around the group, herding them toward the door. Sparrow stuck close to her mom, able to reach out and grab hold of her at any moment.

"I'd like to take Sparrow and leave now," Trudy said as they passed the threshold of the door. The hallway was lit with warm, circular lights embedded in the ceiling. Small, green pulsing lights lined the walls every ten feet or so. The walls were white with a dark red and white lined design running the length.

"You're welcome, by the way," Sulla replied without turning around. She continued walking down the hallway. "You wouldn't even have Sparrow if it wasn't for me. From what I hear, those Flaggers were planning some nasty things for you, Sis."

"Do you want a thank you card? You did what any

decent person would do. You're a saint, Sulla. Congratulations. I'm going now."

Trudy grabbed her daughter's hand and turned, pushing through Teka, Palo, and Rox, determined to find a way out. The security guard stood resolute, blocking the hallway. Sparrow could see behind the security guard, through her legs, and noticed that the door to the small room where they woke up was had disappeared into the wall.

"Move," Trudy said.

The security guard stood still.

"We haven't finished the tour," Sulla said. "You're going to love the tanks."

Sparrow and her mother had no choice but to turn around and follow the procession down the hallway. Trudy kept looking around, trying to find a side hallway or doorway to duck into, but there were none. Sparrow stayed close to her mother's side.

They walked five minutes or so before coming to a stop. Sulla addressed the group.

"As you saw from the control room, Ravenden is home to thousands of people. This facility has many floors underground that look exactly like what you're about to see. Our immersion tanks are custom designed for each user to maximize comfortability and to limit demersion."

"Demersion?" Sparrow asked.

"It's when you have to come out of The Stream," Rox replied, "like to fix your tank or something."

"That's right," Sulla replied. "We take care of the maintenance here. Ravenden has a point zero-zero-zero-one demersion rate here. That's three customers in the past year that had to leave their tank, two of which were able to return less than a minute later."

"Trax," Sparrow said to herself. "Where is Trax?"

"Ah," Sulla said. "Yes, him. Well, he hasn't paid his dues in quite some time. With the condition he's in, we had to move him to the medical wing in the basement."

"I want to see him," Sparrow replied.

"After our little tour. I think you'll love this."

The wall behind Sulla slid open revealing a doorway. Sparrow jolted back a half-step, but the technology here was captivating, especially compared to her life in the castle. Sulla led them into the massive room and spoke, her voice echoing off the high ceilings.

"This is Sanctuary One. Go look around, just don't touch anything." The last sentence had an edge to it, but the group obeyed and slowly fanned out and walked between the caskets. Each tank was a marble sarcophagus, sterile and without blemish. There were no wires or cords or anything coming from the tank. A single gold bar protruded from the case, which Sparrow assumed was the handle.

"Don't touch that," Trudy's voice echoed through the room. Sparrow pulled her hand back.

"I thought you might be interested," Sulla said.

"No," Trudy replied. Sparrow looked at her mom, not sure what was going on.

"She's never been in. Let her see how talented you are," Sulla continued.

"That's not what talent is for," Trudy replied. "We've

played your games. You've done well for yourself. Good for you. Now let us go."

"Sparrow, do you want to see what The Stream is like?" Sulla ignored her sister and turned to her niece.

"We do," Palo said. "It's good seeing you, Sulla, and all that, but we just need to connect so we can get our home back online."

"Palo. Palo. Palo," Sulla said. "Nothing below the surface." Sulla motioned to the security guard. "Take them to the temporary tanks." The security guard motioned for them to follow her, and Teka and Palo started on their way.

"Rox," Teka said, after taking a few steps.

"I..." Rox started, "I want to stay with Sparrow."

"Guess it can't hurt," Teka replied after a moment. "Show her around The Stream a bit. We'll come get you before we go."

Then, without saying goodbye, they were gone.

Only Sulla, Trudy, Rox, and Sparrow stood in Sanctuary One.

"It won't hurt," Sulla spoke.

"I don't need you telling me what will and what won't hurt my daughter. We've been doing just fine without you, without The Stream. Not to mention ten seconds in there will scramble her brain from over-stimulation. She's not ready and she doesn't need it."

"There hasn't been vertigo in years," Sulla laughed. "We've made major upgrades. She won't even notice she's in The Stream."

"Won't notice?" It was Trudy's turn to laugh. "We were decades away from realistic rendering."

Sulla smiled and paused a moment before turning back to Sparrow.

"What do you think? Want to see what it feels like to sail a boat on the ocean?"

Sparrow froze. The last thing she wanted to do was be defiant, but she always dreamed of going into The Stream. She wondered what the ocean was like, how saltwater mist on her face felt.

She didn't reply.

"Let us go," Trudy said, breaking the silence.

"I'll stay with her," Rox said. "Won't take her to see the dinosaurs or to Mars or anything. No war stuff, either."

Trudy turned to her daughter and held her shoulders. "This thing I created, it's not real."

"I know," Sparrow replied.

Trudy grabbed Sparrow's hand. "This is real. This matters."

"I know, Mom," Sparrow replied.

"We're leaving as soon as you're done," Trudy said to her daughter before turning to Sulla. "Ten minutes."

"Ten minutes?" Sulla replied. "That's a lifetime. These tanks are full, of course." Sulla said. "We've got two in Sanctuary Four. Follow me."

The wall slid open revealing a door. Sulla led them inside. As soon as they were in, the floor began to drop and the opening to Sanctuary One rose out of sight. The ceiling emitted a warm glow, despite there being no lights. The walls were some kind of green marble with white swirls. Sulla kept her eyes locked on Trudy.

"What?" Trudy replied.

"It's been too long, Sister. We can't keep doing this. We can't." Sulla broke the stare and looked down to the floor. Sparrow and Rox exchanged sideways glances. Sulla spoke and startled the two girls. "I've got it."

"We're not staying here, Sulla," Trudy replied.

"There's plenty of space. You and Sparrow can have a tank in my private quarters up on the top floor. It'll be just like that little sky cabin you've been living in. We'll have a window installed."

"No," Trudy replied. The elevator slowed.

"I know you don't have any money. Don't worry about it. Ravenden will cover the expenses. It will be nothing. You'll have access to everything you need in The Stream. Sparrow can get some culture. She can make some friends."

"Is this it?" Trudy replied as the elevator door opened to another large room with high ceilings and rows of silver tanks. Sulla clenched her teeth and left the elevator.

"I don't think I'd much like living here," Sparrow said in a low voice.

"I bet my mom and dad would stay, especially if it was free," Rox replied. "We'd all be together then, as a family."

"I guess," Sparrow replied.

"Think it over," Sulla said, voice echoing throughout the room. She motioned to an open tank with the top folded off. "Here we are. Come lay down, Sparrow."

Sparrow looked to her mother for comfort, but the bald woman's eyes remained cold. Sparrow approached the tank. The interior was deep brown leather, the color of Sparrow's helmet. White thread outlined the cushions.

"Are you going to put that thing in my arm?" Sparrow asked. There was an itch in the crease of her elbow.

"Oh, no, no. You won't be in that long."

"Okay."

Sparrow stepped up the small stairs and laid flat in the tank. The black ceiling was all she could see.

"I'll be right here, Sparrow," her mother said, looking over the edge of the tank. "Rox, keep it simple."

"Yes, ma'am." Rox's voice was faint.

"Are you going to hook things to my head now?" Sparrow said as she rubbed the scar on her head.

"Oh, darling," Sulla laughed. "We're not experimenting on you. You've watched too many old movies. When I close the lid, you'll fall asleep, and the tank will connect automatically."

Somehow, that was no more comforting than if there were wires connected to Sparrow's head.

"See you soon," Sulla said as she closed the lid to the tank. The dark ceiling was replaced by the darkness of the tank. An electric whirring filled Sparrow's ears, but it faded as she fell into a deep sleep.

SEVENTEEN

The darkness was replaced by instant, white hot sun. Sparrow's skin felt tight with burning. A stale breeze flecked sand at her face. When she opened her eyes, she stood on a wave of sand, an ocean of brown expanding as far as she could see. Rox stood next to her, smiling.

"Your mom said to take it easy at first. I figured the Sahara Desert wouldn't be too stimulating for you."

"It's so hot," Sparrow said, shielding her eyes. Only then did she realize something had changed. "My hand isn't broken."

"I didn't think you wanted a broken hand in The Stream," Rox replied. "The Stream connects to the brain, so I just bypassed the part where your hand is broken. I can change it back if you'd like."

"No, no. This is good," Sparrow said, squeezing and releasing a fist. "It is so hot, though."

"It's a desert. I can turn the heat intensity down if you'd like."

"But it's not real. This is The Stream."

"Yeah," Rox replied.

"It feels the same as when we were standing in Ravenden. The sounds and feels and smells. Nothing is... less."

"Welcome to The Stream." There was a pause. Sparrow continued to survey the desert around her. The silence was interrupted by an excited whinny. Sparrow jumped and turned to the sound.

"A horse!" she yelled.

"Figured you didn't want to walk," Rox replied. "And this isn't just any horse. This is Blueskin."

"Hercules Adams' horse?" Sparrow said, mouth hanging open. She extended her hand. "Can I?"

"He won't bite."

Sparrow approached the giant steed. Its matte black hair was in brilliant contrast with the dull surroundings. An equally dark leather saddle was strapped to his back. The curvature of the muscles on his thighs shimmered in the sunlight, and veins crisscrossed his sturdy legs. Extending from the saddle, out in front of Blueskin was a long wooden rod, bending at the weight of an oil lamp hanging from the end.

"Thought we could go for a ride," Rox said. Sparrow turned from the horse and looked at her cousin in speechless disbelief. "Come on, I'll help you up. You drive."

As they got up into the saddle, Sparrow in front, Rox holding on behind, the sun set over the farthest dune. The sky was now lit with distant oil lamps, and their oil lamp filled their surroundings with dancing orange light.

"Go ahead," Rox said. Sparrow grabbed the reigns. The horse sprung to life and in an instant, they were galloping across a line of sand dunes. Sparrow went to fasten her helmet, but it was already clasped. She covered her eyes, to keep the sand from filling them, and wished she had some goggles. In the next moment, clear fighter pilot goggles were hanging from her neck. She pulled them up over her eyes as they rode through the desert.

"Ready for something else?" Rox yelled from behind Sparrow.

"Okay," Sparrow replied. The horse dissolved into a leather seat; reigns turned into a steering wheel; the heavy breathing of the horse turned into the roar of an engine. The lamp was now a windshield and through the windshield, Sparrow could see concrete streets snake around a mountain pass with deep valleys below.

"What is this?" Sparrow asked. A car sped around and passed them.

"A race, and now we're losing," Rox laughed. Sparrow pushed the gas pedal slightly, and they sped up. Two more cars sped past. "We can't get hurt."

"Oh," Sparrow replied.

"You don't have to drive so safe. Nothing can hurt us here. Watch." Rox grabbed the steering wheel and jerked the car to the right, off the road, off a cliff.

Sparrow screamed.

The ground grew bigger and bigger until it stopped. It started shrinking. They were no longer in a car falling to their death, but in a hot air balloon rising into the clouds. They passed through a layer of clouds, and the ground vanished.

"Don't do that," Sparrow said, sitting in the corner of the basket.

"Didn't mean to scare you," Rox replied. "Thought you might like this one."

Sparrow got to her feet and gasped at the sight of white clouds floating all around them.

"It's kind of like your paramotor."

"Thanks, Rox," Sparrow replied. "Mom never let me go this high."

"Want to go higher?"

"How high can we go?"

Rox flashed an ornery grin. The flame above them roared to life. The clouds became a snowscape viewed from a mountain peak. All around them the light blue turned purple then black. Sparrow's legs wobbled as she peered over the basket.

"Rox," she mumbled.

"It's safe, Sparrow," Rox replied. "Isn't it beautiful?"

Sparrow looked down at the shrinking blue pebble and the tension left her shoulders. The world popped against the canvas of stars. They floated farther and farther away. Sparrow furled her brows.

"What is it?" Rox asked.

"It just feels strange," Sparrow replied. "This isn't anything like space travel I've read about."

"Oh," Rox replied. "How's this?" In an instant the basket walls grew and enclosed them before turning solid and expanding. Seats popped up from below them and they were clothed in puffy white spacesuits. Sparrow sat at the helm with multicolored, buttons lighting up the dash surrounding her. Rox sat beside her. Deep space filled the glass windshield as the entire cabin rumbled from the rockets.

"Better?" Rox asked.

"I definitely feel safer," Sparrow laughed. "Are we going to the moon?"

"I think time's almost up, so I wanted to show you my favorite place."

"The moon?"

"Mars," Rox replied. "I don't think you want to wait the six months it would usually take, so I sped us up a little." Rox gestured to the window. "What do you think?"

The blue pebble had been replaced by a red rusted stone. It grew and grew until they were speeding into its atmosphere. Alarms beeped and the cabin shook as they made their descent. Moments later the ground was in full view, and they slowed until they hit with a gentle bump. Rox pulled on her helmet.

"Let's go," she said as she ran to the back of the ship. Sparrow followed, lifting the glass bowl over her head. The door to the back of the ship slid open to reveal a brown wasteland, dotted with hills and valleys.

"It looks like the first place we went," Sparrow said, "like the desert."

"Oh," Rox replied. "I guess so. I haven't showed you the best part yet. Follow me."

Rox took off running toward a collection of white rocks. Sparrow followed. As they came nearer to the rocks, Sparrow saw they were not rocks at all. They looked like igloos.

"People live here?" Sparrow asked.

"They were," Rox replied. "Or, did. No, they almost did."

"What?"

"All countries came together to start this settlement. There were big plans. These huts were only the beginning. But, by the time this community started thriving, and were ready for the next round of people, the VR-Evolution hit. The project was abandoned."

"What about the people living here?" Sparrow asked.

"A ship was sent, and they went home. They live in The Stream now, too."

"Oh," Sparrow replied. "And this is your favorite spot in The Stream? Seems a bit, I don't know, depressing."

"You're right," Rox laughed. "That's not why it's my favorite part of The Stream. This is." As she spoke, the sky turned a light blue. The red dirt turned green, as grass sprouted through it. Wildflowers of all kinds colored the rolling hills. The dust-weathered igloos turned to glass roofed domes. The valley filled with water and the sound of a trickling stream filled the air. Rox took off her helmet and filled her lungs with a deep breath. Sparrow did the same.

"It looks just like Earth," Sparrow said.

"Yes," Rox said.

"I don't understand," Sparrow replied.

"I love it here because it's the last time humans dreamed a big dream. Colonizing Mars!" Rox shouted, arms spread wide. "These were the plans. This is what it would have been like. Look what we could do."

"It's not too late for this," Sparrow said.

"I hope not," Rox replied. She knelt and picked a thick-stemmed flower with purple petals and a white center. "We should probably get back."

"Can I take us somewhere?" Sparrow asked.

"Yes! I'd love that," Rox replied. "All you have to do is imagine it."

Sparrow closed her eyes and took a deep breath. A gentle breeze brushed across her face and held locks of her hair suspended. Her body began to bob up and down to the rhythm of creaks, like from an old wooden piano. When Sparrow peeked at her surroundings, her mouth hung open in a joyous gape.

"The Pacific Ocean?" Rox asked.

"I don't know," Sparrow replied. "Just...an ocean." She turned and faced the rising sun, coming up over the salt-water horizon, turning the sky from the midnight blackness to a warm pink. The boat was a small wooden sloop with one sail catching the wind. Sparrow laid on her back in the floor of the boat and looked up to the fading stars.

Sparrow could tell Rox was about to speak, but only the sound of the water carrying the boat remained. Sparrow felt the muscles in her shoulders relax as the small waves gave her an aquatic massage. She was at the will of the ocean, and let it carry her wherever it chose.

After a short while, the sun had risen, but the sky grew dark in a hurry. The next thing Sparrow knew, water dripped from her face, she gasped for breath, and her mother stood above her.

"That's enough."

Sparrow and Rox were helped out of The Stream by some facility personnel who provided towels and a fresh set of clothes. They were then escorted up to Sulla's office on the top floor. When they entered, they quickly realized it was much more than an office.

"Welcome home," Sulla said. "I mean, welcome to my home."

"I thought you said we were going to your office?" Sparrow asked.

"We are," Sulla replied.

"Typical," Trudy said from the back of the group. "Could never separate work and play."

"Oh, that's not it, Sister," Sulla replied. "My work is my play. Unlike you, I love my work."

"Work? Ha," Trudy replied. She sat down on a white leather couch.

"Tell me, Sister, why did you and Teka create FerVR? Why were you obsessed with pushing the limits of virtual reality?"

"I'll play along," Trudy replied. Sulla sat in an oversized chair across from her sister. Sparrow and Rox looked at each other and shrugged before joining Trudy on the couch. "It's the same answer any creator would give; because we have to do it."

"Did you love the work?" Sulla asked.

"Did I love meetings and paperwork? Of course not."

"But did you—"

"When it was just me in my dorm room, programming for 70 hours straight, running scenarios, pushing the boundaries of what would become The Stream, I didn't want anything else."

"There it is," Sulla replied. "I'm responsible for these people. I check in on them, make sure they have everything they want. These people have a life because of what I do here. But it's more than that. The checking in on them, the relationships, the maintenance, I love it all. That's the difference between us."

Trudy didn't answer. Her eyes locked on Sulla. Sparrow and Rox sat in nervous anticipation. "We're done here." Trudy finally replied. "Come on, Sparrow. We're leaving." Sparrow stood, but Sulla interrupted.

"I thought we could have dinner atop the Eiffel Tower tonight," Sulla replied.

"In The Stream?" Sparrow asked.

Sulla laughed. "Of course, dear. What do you say?"

"Sparrow, now," Trudy replied.

"It's settled then. My assistant will show you to your room so you can get cleaned up, not that it matters. I'll send someone to get you in an hour."

"I don't think so," Trudy replied.

"Be a good sport, Sis," Sulla said. "The prodigal daughter has come home. We must celebrate. Off you go."

The security guard came through the door and grabbed Trudy by the arm, escorting her out of Sulla's quarters. Sparrow and Rox followed behind. This hallway was more elaborately furnished than the first they traveled down near the tanks. Abstract shapes carpeted the floor. Paintings from all eras adorned the walls and chandeliers hung their crystal light every couple of steps.

The prepared room was at the opposite side of the

dead-end hallway. Looking down the corridor, Sparrow could only see Sulla's door and the elevator door at the opposite end. As they approached, their door slid open, and the security guard ushered them inside. The room was decorated just like the hallway and seemed to swallow them up with its tall ceilings and arched doorways. Again, the walls were covered with renaissance-era paintings. There were no windows.

"One hour," the security guard said from the hallway. The door slid closed, melting back into the wall. Trudy examined the door.

"Sealed tight," she said. "Like it's not even there."

"She's not so bad, Mom," Sparrow said.

Trudy turned to her daughter. "You've known her for two hours."

"She's been nice to us," Rox added.

"We're prisoners," Trudy replied, raising her voice.

"She misses you," Sparrow added.

"You think forcing us to share a meal makes us family? Holding us hostage will make me love her? That's not how it works." Sparrow and Rox were speechless. Trudy's face relaxed. "I'll play along if it means getting us out of here. Go get cleaned up, you two."

Sparrow and Rox explored the living quarters and found a large open room full of couches and giant bean bags. There was a room with three immersion tanks in a row. Three separate bedrooms, each with their own bathrooms, showers, and wash machines. The girls picked a room. Trudy took the leftover.

"Is this for fish?" Sparrow yelled from her room. Trudy and Rox came in.

"It's for cleaning clothes," Trudy said. "When you're done getting cleaned up, bring your clothes in here and I'll wash them."

Sparrow looked through the dressers at the clothes Sulla had provided, but they were all stiff and cold. She dug through the bottom drawer and found moss-green tights and a long shirt. She left the room with her dirty clothes in a pile. She found Rox digging through a pile of clothes.

"How long does it take that fish tank to wash our clothes?" Sparrow asked.

"Couldn't find anything either?" Rox replied. "Let's try it."

Sparrow threw her clothes in the glass box. Rox did the same.

"Mom," Sparrow yelled. "Want us to put your clothes in this washer thing?"

A few moments later, Trudy came to the door of their room. Her skin shined and her clothes looked brand new. The dirt and blood were gone.

"Way ahead of you," she said. "Better get it going. Jump in the shower and it'll be done when you get out."

The girls did what they were told. Rox got the clothes washer going and Sparrow went back to her room to shower. The water was the perfect temperature. Her shoulders relaxed as the warm water massaged her tense muscles.

Then, without warning, while she was rinsing the soap from her hair, the water turned ice cold and her mind went back to the frigid rain falling on her face in the rail yard. Flashes of the Flagger's bloodied head and lifeless eyes sent a trembling in her legs.

Her foot slipped, sending her backwards, head crashing into the wall. She was in the lake again, sinking to the bottom. Everything went black.

EIGHTEEN

"Sparrow?" an ethereal voice echoed in the darkness. "Wake up."

She opened her eyes to see her mother, Rox, and Sulla standing over her. Sharp pain penetrated her temple when she tried to speak. She reached up to touch it.

"Don't," Trudy said.

"Been that long since you showered?" Sulla said, trying to lighten the mood.

"Your scar," Rox said.

Sparrow realized the pain in her temple was coming from her scar. She reached up for it again.

"No, Sparrow," Trudy said. "What happened?"

"I don't know," Sparrow replied, head still throbbing. "I blacked out and must have fallen."

"You definitely fell," Sulla said. "Cracked your head on the tile. This shot right here should heal you up right away." She lifted a small syringe. "Will make that hand feel better, too."

"I don't think so," Trudy said, grabbing her sister's hand.

"Mom, please," Sparrow said from the couch. "Make it go away."

Sulla looked at Trudy, who let go of her wrist and turned her face away.

"You won't even feel this," Sulla said. "You'll probably feel sleepy. But once you wake up you should be good as new."

Sparrow nodded.

Sulla stuck the needle into Sparrow's neck.

Sparrow winced and passed out.

SHE WOKE in what felt like a blink of an eye. The slight pressure from the bandage wrapped around her head was the only thing she felt. The sharp pain was gone. The throbbing was gone. She thought about calling out to her mother but decided to try to get up on her own.

She leaned forward slowly, feeling slight vertigo. There was no way to know how long she'd been out.

"You're awake," Rox yelled from the foot of the couch.

Sparrow jumped. "You scared me."

"Sorry," Rox replied. "How is it?"

"Gone," Sparrow said. "Feels like nothing happened."

"What did happen in there?"

"Where's Mom and Sulla?" Sparrow said.

"Your mom's in her room. I think Sulla left," Rox replied.

"Okay, well, when I was in the shower the face of the Flagger I killed came to mind and caught me off-guard. I must have fainted."

"Why didn't you say that earlier?"

"I can't tell my mom that I'm a killer," Sparrow said. "I killed someone, Rox." Tears began to fill her eyes and run down her cheeks.

"You didn't mean to do it," Rox replied.

Sparrow's tears were hot streams now. "What should I say? 'Oh, by the way, Mom, when I was looking for you with my family you never told me about, I was almost killed in a dirty sewer under the city, but instead I used the skills you gave me and cracked open some lady's skull. Aren't you proud?'"

"Sparrow," Rox said, as gently as possible. "I'm just glad you're okay now."

Sparrow sniffed and tried to compose herself.

"When they brought you out here, your head was bleeding so much. I thought you were gone."

"I'm sorry," Sparrow sniffled.

"It's okay. Just don't go get yourself hurt, okay? We got to stick together."

Sparrow nodded.

Before they could say another word, the door slid open, and Sulla came inside.

"Just wanted to—oh good! You're awake," she said as she walked over to Sparrow. "How are you feeling?"

"Better," Sparrow replied. "Perfect, really. Even my hand feels better. I can move my fingers a little."

"Amazing technology, isn't it? It's like reprograming the pain to go somewhere else." Sulla laughed. Sparrow and Rox stared at her. Trudy entered the room.

"Sparrow," she said as she rushed to her daughter. "Well?"

"All better," Sparrow replied.

"Wonderful, isn't it?" Sulla interrupted. "I guess that means we're ready for dinner. Follow me."

"Give us a minute," Trudy said. "We're not even dressed."

Sulla gave a stern look, but it only lasted a moment. Her eyes softened as she smiled. "Come to my room when you're ready."

Trudy nodded and Sulla left the room.

"I thought we weren't dressing up," Sparrow asked.

"We're not," her mother replied. "We're leaving."

"What about me?" Rox asked. Trudy turned to her niece with her lips pursed.

"Can she come with us?" Sparrow asked.

Before Trudy could reply, Rox spoke again. "And leave my parents here?"

"We can bring you back to your house once everything gets fixed," Sparrow replied.

"Oh," Rox said. "It's not that."

"We've got to go now, girls," Trudy said. "Rox, you're welcome to come with us so you know where the exit is, just in case."

Rox nodded. They grabbed what little personal items they had and made for the door. It slid open and they walked toward Sulla's room. The elevator door was just beyond Sulla's door. Trudy whispered, "Stay close."

As they strode passed the door to Sulla's penthouse,

they sped up to reach the elevator. Trudy smashed the button and the doors opened. Once inside, Sparrow remembered there were no buttons on the control panel. It was activated by Sulla's face recognition.

"Mom," Sparrow whispered.

"Quiet," Trudy whispered as she took a fork from her pocket. She pried off the metal casing around the control panel. Behind the metal shield lay a spiderweb of wires and blinking lights. Sparrow saw her mother reach inside and unplug and reconnect wires. Rox stared at her cousin in disbelief. Sparrow shrugged her shoulders.

After thirty seconds of the madness, the elevator door slid closed, and they began to ascend.

"No," Trudy cursed. "Down."

She dove back into the exposed mechanical control panel as the elevator took them higher and higher. There were no numbers. No lights. No indication of how high they were. Then, with a jolt, they stopped. A bell rang, and the door slid open.

A gust of wind invaded the small elevator. It carried snowflakes on its wings and howled like a tornado. They stepped outside and found themselves on a platform no bigger than the first floor of the castle. A half-wall edged the concrete floor, but there was no ceiling above; only the swirling clouds looking the same concrete grey as what was below their feet.

They were on the roof.

Trudy looked over the edge and cursed.

"Snow?" Rox asked.

"We must be as high as the mountains," Sparrow replied.

"Get back in the elevator," Trudy growled. The girls got back inside as Trudy took another look at the control panel. Just before she reached her hands inside, the elevator door slammed shut and they began a quick descent.

"Too fast," Rox said, shaking.

"Mom," Sparrow plead.

"It's not me," Trudy replied, now tinkering with the control panel. "Nothing is working."

The elevator began to slow. Trudy faced the door and corralled the girls behind her. They rolled to a stop. A moment passed. Then, another. Sparrow peeked around her mother in anguished expectancy, but the door remained shut. Sparrow looked at Rox, who returned her look with an equally puzzled expression. Trudy took a step to the control panel and the door slid open in a fury, revealing the hallway they had just exited.

Sulla stood with arms folded and teeth clenched.

The security guard stood behind her holding a police baton.

"Did you forget which room was mine?" Sulla's voice filled the elevator like a screeching squall.

"Let us leave," Trudy demanded.

"It's time for dinner," Sulla said. She exited the hall into her room. A moment later the security guard approached the open elevator. She reached out to grab Trudy's arm, but Sparrow's mother swatted it away.

"Do that again and it'll be broken in more places than you can count," she roared. "Stay close, girls."

Sparrow and Rox huddled behind Trudy as they exited the elevator and entered Sulla's quarters.

"Ah, glad you all could make it," Sulla remarked in an airy falsetto. She sat at the head of a large wooden table that had not been in the apartment on their first tour. "I see you're still wearing your old-world rags. Didn't like the attire I provided?"

"Let's get this over with," Trudy replied.

"Please, please. Have a seat."

Trudy sat at the opposite end of her sister. Sparrow and Rox sat opposite of each other. An enormous chandelier with flickering candles hung over the table. Small potted ferns filled the corners of the room. Exotic vines with flowers of every color lined the giant window at the end of the room behind Sulla. The sky was full of brilliant hues of purple and orange as the sun set below the mountains.

A small bird flew from a tree in the back of the room to a larger one in the front, near the windows. The guests all stared and whipped their heads to follow the bird in flight.

"Isn't it wonderful?" Sulla said as the bird found a branch near the window. "Sometimes I sit in here when I've got a problem to solve, or a big decision to make. It makes me smile."

Sparrow kept her eye on the little bird and watched as it hopped around on a branch, looking out through the window at the open air.

"Do you have a happy place, Sparrow?" Sulla continued.

"Oh," Sparrow said, looking from the bird to her aunt. "I can see the top of the trees from my room at home. I like that."

"That's nice," Sulla replied. "I would ask you, Sister, but you might have a hard time remembering the last time you were actually happy." She laughed to herself. No one else did. The bird hopped up to a higher branch and put its beak to the glass.

"Let me and my daughter out of your private fantasy. Let us go home," Trudy said again, looking down the table at her sister. "That'll make me happy."

"How long has it been?" Sulla replied. "How old are you, Sparrow?"

"Fifteen."

"My goodness," Sulla replied. "Then it's been..."

"Eleven years," Trudy grumbled.

"That's right. I was still living with Mom and Dad," Sulla said. "You know, Dad went looking for you."

"Stop," Trudy said.

"I told him you were a grown woman and that he was going to get hurt out there," Sulla went on. "Two years after you went off the grid, he couldn't take it anymore. He went looking for you."

"Don't."

"We found him nine months later curled up in a shallow cave, cuts and bruises marring his face and limbs, repeating your name over and over." Trudy stood up from the table in a hurry. She walked to the door, but it was gone. She stood with her back to the table. "I built this place for him, you know." Sulla went on. "Mom, too."

Trudy turned and faced the group. Her eyes red. Sulla delivered the final blow.

"They died three months ago."

Sparrow could see her mother's legs trembling. Trudy shuffled back to her seat and collapsed into it just in time. She dropped her head into her hands. A dull clicking sound thumped from the window. Sparrow turned to see the bird pecking at the glass.

"They were happy in The Stream. Dad could only function in there. We had to remap his tank to bypass the trauma and dementia. It was successful for the most part. When I would check in on them, he'd always be reliving the same night."

"Christmas," Trudy wept.

"I don't think I can remember it for myself. Everything I know about it is from living it over and over in The Stream. He loved watching your face light up when you opened–"

"The Python starter set," Trudy said. "He knew how much I wanted to learn to code."

"I think I got a sweatshirt," Sulla replied.

"You were four," Trudy said.

"And an accident," Sulla said. It was her turn to stand up. She looked out of the window. "It was already hard for them to get out of bed by the time they had me. Dad never rolled around on the ground with me. They always talked about FerVR and how proud they were of you two." Sulla turned back to the table now, but Trudy spoke first.

"They loved you."

"I raised myself," she walked back to her seat. "Once The Stream was up, we were one of the first ones in. Mom and Dad had all their strength back. We were invincible. We could do anything; could go anywhere."

She dropped her head and stared at the floor. Her black hair hung down over her face. "But every day was Christmas. Always Christmas."

"What do you want me to do?" Trudy asked. Sulla ignored her and went on.

"I knew this was going to be big, so I used Mom and Dad's savings and bought our first facility. Nothing like this," she laughed as she motioned to the room. "Small. Thirty residents, including Mom and Dad. Wasn't long until we were pushing a thousand, five thousand residents. They were begging for a tank. People had sold their cars, their houses. They were betting it all on your little invention. I was determined to use it to benefit Mom and Dad. That's what I did. They always had the best tanks."

Sulla sat back down at the table and adjusted her cutlery before continuing.

"So, I guess in a way, thank you. I couldn't have done it without my sisters."

"What happened to Mom and Dad," Trudy asked, hands trembling.

"No," Sulla said, voiced raised. "You don't get to care now."

"I always cared," Trudy replied, matching the volume.

"Words," Sulla said. "Just words."

"Sulla." Trudy said in an even voice. "What happened–"

"I told you," Sulla erupted. "Dad went crazy. He got some disease from being outside and never fully recovered. Once he was gone, Mom followed right after.

She couldn't stand it." Sulla began to shout. "Or do you mean the bodies? What happened to the lifeless bodies of our parents? You want to see them now?" She paused. Not expecting an answer. "No!" she yelled. "You don't get that."

"Sulla," Trudy replied through tears.

"No!" Sulla snapped back. "This is what you get."

As she spoke those words, the wall behind Rox slid up and out of sight, revealing a small room with two silver immersion tanks side by side. The light from the chandelier reflected off the smooth, mirrored exterior. The coffins had iron bolts the size of Sparrow's hands lining the exterior, connecting the lid and the base, sealing them shut.

"I never realized how much they do look like coffins," Sulla said, tears now rolling down her cheeks. Trudy sobbed. Sparrow and Rox were crying, too.

Trudy stood and approached the tanks.

"I don't think so," Sulla said. The door from the hallway slid open and the security guard came in and grabbed Trudy's arm before she could take a step. "In fact, I'm not very hungry anymore. Take them away."

The security guard grabbed Trudy and Sparrow. Rox followed behind and Sulla continued.

"And lock the bald one in a tank. I want her to see the cave where we found Dad."

NINETEEN

Sparrow and Rox were led back into the room where they had spent the hour getting ready before dinner. Trudy was still being held by the security guard, but she wasn't resisting. She looked at her daughter, tears filling both eyes, as the door slid shut between them.

"Mom!' Sparrow yelled. She dug her fingernails into the wall where the door was, but it wouldn't budge. She lifted a stool from the bar and rammed it into the door to no avail. The wooden stool vibrated in her hands from the impact. She dropped it to the floor and wept in pain.

Collecting herself, she bent down to pick it up, but she couldn't.

"Sparrow," Rox said, holding the stool to the floor. "Don't hurt yourself."

"I won't lose her again," Sparrow cried.

"You won't," Rox replied. "She won't hurt your mom. They're sisters."

Sparrow wasn't fully convinced, but her sobs turned to whimpers as she let Rox lead her to the couch.

"She's probably hurting her," Sparrow said. "She hates my mom."

"Your mom is strong. She survived being stranded outside and captured by Flaggers. Not to mention raising a daughter in the woods all these years."

Sparrow looked up from the floor. "This is different," she replied.

"You seemed to turn out okay," Rox said with a grin.

"What do you think she's doing to her?" Sparrow asked, turning her gaze to the window.

"Sounded like she was taking her to the tanks. Putting her in The Stream to see her dad."

"It can't hurt her, though, right?"

"Not physically," Rox replied. "Long term anyway." The implications of her answer hung in the room. The sun was shining again through the window. The trees below appeared as clovers in grass from this height.

"We've got to do something," Sparrow said. "There must be a way out of here. We're missing something."

"I'll grab our bags," Rox replied as she left the couch. Sparrow paced in front of the window until Rox returned.

"If only Hobbes were here," Sparrow said. "We could get plans for this building, or even send it to explore for us. To be our eyes."

"Oh," Rox said. "Try Watzon again."

"I've tried everything. All diagnostics say it should be working. No errors. But I can't get a response."

"Come on," Rox replied, handing Sparrow her bag. "It's our best chance."

Sparrow took the bag and dug around inside. She reached around, expecting to hit the metal ball almost immediately in the bottom of the small bag. There was nothing. She turned the backpack upside-down and dumped its contents on the couch in a frenzy.

"It's gone," Sparrow said.

"What?" Rox replied.

"She took it," Sparrow went on. "After they knocked us out. Make sure you have everything else."

They spent the next few minutes going their personal belongings. They found their hats, gloves, scarves, and cans of artichoke hearts exactly how they'd left them.

Sparrow lifted the bird pocket watch necklace from inside her shirt and exhaled slowly when she found it completely intact. She pushed the button on the side, but it wouldn't open. The weight of it in her hand sparked a chain of memories that jumped and skipped from the pocket watch to the barn to the wagon to the train yard.

"Trax!" Sparrow yelled.

"He could help us," Rox replied. "He's been here before."

"That must be why they took him."

"Sulla said they're taking care of him."

"Why didn't Sulla let us see him?"

"I don't know," Rox replied.

"I'm terrible," Sparrow said, collapsing on the couch. "I was so taken in by The Stream I forgot about him."

"You got him here," Rox replied. "You kept your promise."

"Maybe," Sparrow said. "I told him I would take him to the lake, too, but that's not going to happen."

"He's probably just resting."

"I have to see him," Sparrow replied. She got up and went back to the sliding door and began pounding her fists against the metal. "I want to see Trax," she yelled.

Nothing happened.

"Let me see my friend," she went on.

Still nothing.

This went on for a long time. After an hour or so, she fell asleep at the foot of the door. She was jolted awake by the sliding door. She looked up and saw Sulla standing in the void.

"Follow me." Sparrow got to her feet. Rox pulled herself from the couch. The girls followed their aunt into the elevator at the end of the hall. Sulla spoke as the elevator doors slid shut.

"I have to warn you, he's not well."

The elevator purred as they descended. A thousand questions swirled in Sparrow's mind, but she couldn't bring herself to ask one. She knew she wouldn't believe Sulla, no matter what she said. It had to be with her own eyes. She had to see for herself.

The small room eased to a stop, but the doors remained closed.

"I'm sorry, Sparrow. He—"

"I want to see him."

Sulla nodded and the doors split open. Sparrow had yet to see this floor. Fluorescent lights lined the hallway.

The ground was polished concrete. Doorways like open wounds dotted the corridor. The walls were pale white like melting snow.

"What is this?" Rox asked.

"Medical floor," Sulla replied. "We've got a doctor on staff. Usually, she can monitor patients in The Stream, no big deal. Occasionally, though, we need complete demersion to address a health concern. Used to have to fly people up to St. Louis. Now they can stay here."

"It's a prison," Sparrow said.

"Well, we don't want them to get too comfortable here." Sulla left the elevator. Sparrow and Rox followed.

"Where is he?"

"Not very patient, are we?" Sulla replied. "Just in here. Room two."

"Wait," Sparrow said. "I'd like to go in alone, if that's okay."

"No problem at all," Sulla said.

"I was asking Rox."

Rox gave a half-grin before replying with a half-committed, "Okay."

Sparrow stepped forward and crossed the threshold into the poorly lit room. It was a perfect square with a bed on one wall and a toilet and bathtub on another. A blanketed shadow lay in the bed, complete with an oxygen mask with one blinking white light.

"Trax?" Sparrow's voice broke.

The head of the body moved side to side. A quick exhale turned to a cough, which turned into a full-blown wheezing bout. The man pulled the mask from his face and Sparrow saw a pair of eyes darker than the room which they stood. But they were eyes of a friend.

"I thought you left me," Trax said in a jovial voice incongruent with the content spoken. "Wouldn't blame you. Got to throw the excess weight overboard."

"I didn't," Sparrow pleaded. "They attacked us. Knocked us out."

"Never trust a suit," Trax said.

"We woke up here," Sparrow continued. "Did they hurt you?"

"Hurt me?" Trax said before giving a deep belly laugh. "They've helped me. Gave me meds and let me stay here."

Sparrow looked around the plain room.

"It beats dying alone," Trax replied.

"So, you're okay?" Sparrow asked.

"Relatively speaking."

"What does that mean?"

"Well," Trax took a deep breath before continuing. "This visor here let me access The Stream in a limited way. I got to see my family. Tell them I was hurt. Say my goodbyes."

"What?" Sparrow jolted up in her chair.

"I'm not the hopeful type. I see two legs bloodied and mangled, and I know it won't be long before I go back to the dust."

"No," Sparrow whimpered.

"Hell, I thought I'd be long gone by now. Just a body in the wide-open world. You kept me going. You brought me here so I could see my family again. I can't thank you enough for doing that."

"They can help you," Sparrow said. "They've got a doctor here. Fancy medicine to heal you up."

"Doc says it's infected. Already spread up my belly and all around my heart."

Sparrow sat back in her chair, trying to focus on the secret plan her and Rox had made. Seeing Trax brought out too many emotions. She just wanted to check on her friend, to make sure he was alright, but there was something she had to do. She clenched her fist as she spoke.

"There was only one place you wanted to go, and I promised I would take you there. Remember?"

"You've done more than enough, Sparrow."

"I told you I'd take you to the top of the mountain, so you could see the longest sunset."

"It's okay," Trax replied. "I'll just have to go in The Stream and pretend it's the real thing."

Sparrow dropped her head and gave a whimper to feign crying, but her brain was working overtime. She had a strange feeling something was wrong, and this confirmed it. The dots began to connect. She came to the realization that they had done something to Trax. This wasn't her friend.

With that revelation, a wave of fear rushed over her like a warm summer rain. She was in danger.

"What is it?" Trax asked.

"Just picturing taking you up to the mountain by my house," Sparrow replied.

"Why don't you hop in The Stream, and you can show me? Bring your mom and Rox, too."

"Yeah," Sparrow replied. "I hadn't thought of that."

She stood in front of his bed, trying to find the words that would release her from this moment. She was saved when the gravel voice spoke.

"Thanks for coming down here. I know it ain't pretty."

"I'm sorry it took so long," Sparrow replied.

"Ah," he growled. "You've got nothing to be sorry for."

"I'll come see you again soon," Sparrow replied.

"I'd like that," Trax replied. "Goodbye, Sparrow."

Sparrow left the room and returned to her aunt and cousin. Their soft voices faded in reverence when Sparrow approached. She was unaware her face showed the bewilderment puzzling her thoughts. It was evident when Sulla broke the silence.

"What's wrong?" Sulla asked.

"I don't want to talk about it. I'd like to go back to my room," Sparrow replied, eyes still downcast. She didn't dare meet the eyes of the Roark of Ravenden, the woman in charge of this whole facility, while the spark of defiance started within her.

Sulla nodded and led the girls back to the elevator and to their room. The sun still shone through the windows, and the clouds passed by their high-rise apartment as they entered. Sulla paused for a moment, then left the room, door disappearing behind her.

"We need to hurry," Sparrow said after checking the door.

"What?" Rox said in surprise. "You were just moping around. Is it Trax?"

"I can't say anymore," Sparrow replied. "Tell me about The Stream. Is it hard to track people in there?"

"Sparrow—"

"Please, Rox," Sparrow whispered.

"It depends on your privacy settings," Rox replied. "You can choose who sees you. And, well, there's one place where no tracking is allowed."

"Where?"

"It's called Hoffgrid. It's dangerous, people can steal your–"

"What about at higher levels? Like, the people who keep The Stream going?"

"The Stream was made public decades ago. No one owns it."

While Rox spoke, Sparrow stood in front of the window looking out over the landscape. "Once it was made public, everyone could access any data that was being stored. People got upset. Now it's government-funded, but no information is stored anywhere."

"What about facilities? Like Ravenden?"

"I'm not sure," Rox replied. "We've always had our own tanks. I suppose they could."

"Take me there," Sparrow replied, making her way to the immersion tanks in the room.

"Where?" Rox asked, horrified.

"Back to The Stream."

They lifted the tank lids. Rox helped Sparrow get in first, before getting in her own tank. The world went dark. Sparrow took a deep breath, counted to ten, and opened her eyes. She stood at the base of a hundred-year-old oak tree with a tire swing hanging from one of its branches. Grass rolled over the hills like an emerald ocean. Rox swung back and forth on the tire swing.

"You beat me here?" Sparrow asked.

"I'm pretty good at immersion. Been doing it my whole life." She dug her heels into the dirt and came to a stop. "What now?"

"I want to see all The Stream has to offer. I barely got my feet wet before. Show me more," Sparrow replied. "I just need to take my mind off everything."

"Where to?" Rox replied.

Sparrow paused. She knew it probably wasn't safe here and didn't want to raise any suspicions. She had a plan, but she needed to execute it slowly.

"Hobbes was closed circuit. Only had info up to about a decade ago. Show me what I've missed since then," Sparrow said.

"I can do that," Rox replied with enthusiasm.

Rox motioned for Sparrow to follow her. As they ran around the tree, she saw a large, two-seat paramotor waiting in the grass. The deep-violet parachute floated in the wind, even with the top of the tree. They sat side-by-side in mahogany-cushioned recliners.

"Thought you'd be comfortable this way," Rox said.

"It's perfect."

Rox smiled as the paramotor roared to life. They rose above the hills and the sky turned from deep blue to black. Faces and buildings and names lit up the sky like a planetary theater. Rox showed Sparrow the first great immersion, when most of the populace made the plunge into full-time life in The Stream.

As Rox was beginning to share about the second immersion, Sparrow stopped her.

"Can you take me to Hoffgrid?"

"Right now?"

Sparrow nodded.

"I don't know," Rox replied.

"I'd like to see it. I want to get a full experience in The Stream."

"I get that," Rox replied. "It's just not the most welcoming place. It creeps me out."

"We don't have to stay long."

"Fine," Rox replied. "Only for a second, though."

Rox turned the steering wheel of the paramotor and pointed the aircraft to the ground. They landed in the base of a deep canyon. The walls stretched high on either side, closing in on the blue sky.

"Is this it?" Sparrow asked, stepping off the paramotor.

"There," Rox replied, pointing to a dark crack in the wall. The sun washed the valley with warm light, but the hole in the wall was solid black, like an unnatural, vantablack curtain hanging over the entrance. Sparrow walked toward it. Rox grabbed her arm.

"We shouldn't stay long."

"Okay," Sparrow replied.

"I'm serious. If something happens to us in there, no one will know."

"Got it," Sparrow replied, pulling her arm free. She walked toward the darkness, reached her hand in, and stepped through. She stood in a dark void. White numbers flashed in the distance like lightning strikes.

"I thought you said there were people here?"

"We've only just stepped in," Rox replied.

"Numbers?"

"Code. People who hang out in here think it's cool. Like they're seeing behind the curtain. Someone designed it just like that canyon out there." She paused before continuing. "Can we go?"

"No one could collect our information in here?"

"You think someone's spying on us?"

"Could they if we're in here?"

"No." Rox replied. "What's going on?"

"Rox, I think we're already in The Stream."

"Of course, we are!" Rox exclaimed. "Remember the part where we were flying?"

"No, not now," Sparrow replied. "Okay, yes, we're in The Stream now, but I think we've been in The Stream this whole time. Since we got to Ravenden."

"No," Rox replied. "Can't be. I grew up in The Stream. I would know."

"You said it yourself, that The Stream feels realistic."

"Why, though?" Rox asked. "Why would we be in The Stream?"

"Think about it. What does Sulla want more than anything?"

"Her parents?"

"Power," Sparrow replied. "She's always been the youngest. Always having to follow in her sisters' footsteps. She built Ravenden to be in power over everyone inside. Their livelihood depends on her keeping them connected to The Stream. Then, when she found her sisters, she wanted to do the same thing to them."

"That's crazy. If we're in The Stream, I should be able to do all the things I've been doing in here. Like flying and stuff."

"She must be blocking some features or something."

"That doesn't prove anything," Rox replied. "A lot of people want power."

"My pocket watch wouldn't open," Sparrow said.

"Must be jammed," Rox replied.

"I bet they didn't know it opened, so it's not programmed that way."

"I don't know, Sparrow," Rox said.

"It was Trax," Sparrow said in desperation.

"What?"

"When I went to see him. That's how I knew." Sparrow's voice grew softer. "It wasn't him. It couldn't have been."

"Who did you talk to in there?"

"I don't know. It looked like him. And sounded like him. I said I was sorry I didn't take him to the top of the mountains, like he always wanted to do, and he didn't correct me. It wasn't mountains. He wanted to see the lake. He told me when I first met him."

"Maybe he just forgot. He was beat up pretty bad."

"Maybe," Sparrow said unconvincingly. "You know those lights that run the length of the hallways back at Ravenden?"

"The operational ones?"

"That's right. What color are they?"

"Green. We already talked about—" Sparrow could see Rox's eyes open wide as the realization washed over her. "They're...green."

"See?"

"But I'm colorblind. I can't see green."

"Except in The Stream."

"We have to get back. We have to tell my parents. Your mom."

"Hold on," Sparrow grabbed Rox's arm. "We can't let Sulla know, or she'll add extra security."

"But she's watching us constantly."

"I've got an idea," Sparrow said feigning confidence. "Can you encrypt a message?"

TWENTY

As Sparrow lifted the lid to the tank, the apartment, her cage in Ravenden, surrounded her. Before she could lift herself from the tank, a shrill voice filled the room.

"Can't get enough, huh?" Sulla's voice filled the room. She sat semi-reclined on the couch. The security guard stood in the open doorway leading to the hall.

"It's all so interesting," Sparrow replied in her most girlish tone.

"Hmmm," Sulla replied. She sat upright and at attention.

Water from the tank dripped on the floor. Sparrow dried her hair with a nearby towel. Rox did the same. Sulla studied the girls, who stood in her paralyzing gaze. Without warning, the stone-cold eyes flashed with light and a smile broke across Sulla's face as she patted the empty couch beside her.

"Well, tell me all about it."

"I showed her some history," Rox said.

"Exhilarating," Sulla replied sarcastically.

"There's a lot I don't know," Sparrow replied, finding a seat next to her aunt. Rox followed.

"Me too, darling. Me too." Sulla ran her finger along Sparrow's scar. "We've made an interesting history for ourselves. Being so focused on leading the way to the future, we forgot it would all be history someday. What we did and the choices we made, sealed in the stonework of time for all to see."

Sparrow nodded.

"Make the right choice today, and it's cemented in time forever. You can always look back on that day and know you did good. No one can change that. Do you understand, Sparrow?"

"Yes, ma'am," Sparrow replied, unable to avoid proper etiquette when called out by name.

"Very good," Sulla said as she stood. "I'm sure your mother will be joining soon. If you need anything, be sure to let us know. Enjoy The Stream."

"Thank you," Sparrow replied.

Sulla walked through the open door, with the security guard close behind. The Roark stopped in the hallway and looked back at Sparrow with cold, dead eyes.

"Oh, and stay out of Hoffgrid."

With those words, the door slid shut, leaving the warning to echo off the walls of the suite.

Sparrow turned to Rox, whose eyes were now tracing the grout between the tile on the floor. Her lips were pulled tight. Sparrow grabbed her cousin's hand and met her eyes with the most confidence she could muster. She pulled the locket from her neck and held it in front of them.

"Will you hold on to this for me?" she asked.

Rox smiled, teeth reflecting the light from the room. "Of course," she replied. "You'll have it back soon, though."

There was a pause. Both girls locked eyes and gave a slight nod. A newfound resolve filled them.

"I think I'm going to lay down for a bit," Sparrow said. "Not used to all that stimulation from The Stream."

"That?" Rox joked. "The history of The Stream was overstimulating to you? It puts most people to sleep for different reasons." They laughed. "I'm going back in, going to see if I can catch up with some friends."

"Cool," Sparrow replied, lying flat on the couch. "I'll be here."

She turned, facing the back cushion of the couch, and brought her right hand up under her head. Her cheek laid flat on the fabric still stiff and itchy from lack of use. She closed her eyes and her mind exploded with activity. The plan she and Rox had made in Hoffgrid was in motion. Her hand shook with anticipation like the first time she flew solo in the paramotor. So much had to go right. There were far too many opportunities for failure. Now, Rox had been dragged into the mess and it was Sparrow's fault.

A beacon of stillness shown like a tower in her psyche. She pushed through the fear of not seeing her mother again, never leaving Ravenden, and being trapped in the quasi-reality her aunt had built.

Then, silence.

She looked around in her mind's eye and found herself in her bed, with the sun coming up over Reelfoot Lake and the mountains to the east. The smell and sizzle of her mom cooking fish filled her small room. Birds sang outside of her window. A small metal robot sat idle on the charging bay beside her. Her bo staff was nowhere to be found.

She was home.

"Sparrow, get up," a voice called out. Sparrow recognized the voice, but knew it wasn't her mother's. Who else was in the tower? "Sparrow, hurry." The tower faded into deep memory and the itch from the stiff cushion returned. She opened her eyes.

"Sparrow, you've got to go."

It was Rox's amplified voice coming from the ceiling.

She was in.

She hacked The Stream.

Sparrow slid off the couch and crouched behind it. "Sorry, sorry," she whispered. "I'm ready now."

"Biometric duplicate complete," Rox said. "Opening the door now."

"It's clear?" Sparrow replied, approaching the door.

"Of course, it's clear. That's what I'm doing here. You've got to move, though. I don't know how long I have until they kick me off."

Sparrow leaned her head through the doorway into the empty hallway. She made her way to the elevator.

"Not the elevator," the voice said from the ceiling. "Stairs, behind you and to the left. All clear."

Sparrow did an about-face and made her way to the stairs. She hadn't gone down this part of the hallway before. The only two doors were where they had dinner with Sulla and their suite. She made it to the end of the main hall and turned left. Twenty paces later, she came to a glass door with a stairwell on the other side.

"There's no handle," Sparrow said.

"Okay," Rox replied, obviously distracted.

"Why do they need stairs here, if we're in The Stream?"

"Not sure," Rox replied, hardly paying attention. "It looks like they've modeled this virtual Ravenden from the blueprint of the physical facility. There we go." The door slid open. Sparrow had already descended a flight of stairs before the door slid closed.

"We were right. It looks like all outbound interactions have been disabled in this virtual version of Ravenden. That explains why we didn't see any other users when we thought we were accessing The Stream before."

"So, you can't send the message from there?" Sparrow asked, making her way down the stairwell.

"That's right. There's only one computer here with that access." Rox went quiet. Sparrow assumed this would be the case, but the reality didn't ease the pressure of what they had to do.

"Where's her office?" Sparrow asked.

"Fourth floor," the voice echoed in the stairwell. A huge number thirteen was painted red near the door on the landing she just cleared.

"Stop!" Rox yelled. Sparrow froze on the landing between floor twelve and thirteen. "Back up, through the door to the thirteenth floor."

Sparrow opened her mouth to reply, but echoes from a far-off conversation murmured up the concrete stairwell. She stepped quietly back to the thirteenth floor, where the door was waiting open for her. She walked through and it slid shut.

"What's going on?" Sparrow asked, standing in the middle of the hallway.

"I didn't think there was anyone else here. This is a simulation." Rox's voice rang through the hallway.

"Those guards sure sounded real to me," Sparrow replied.

"That doesn't make sense. She can control everything. Monitor any room. Move any walls. She's in control of the whole thing."

"She's trying to keep up the illusion," Sparrow said before her mind caught up. She paused, putting it all together, before continuing. "If we made a run for it, she could send the guards to collect us. But, if she stepped through a wall or something, we'd know something was off."

"They're almost on this floor," Rox replied. "You've got to go."

Sparrow could hear the muffled sound of boots stomping concrete stairs behind the door.

"Waiting for you," Sparrow replied, frustration growing in her voice.

"Find the elevator. Should be around the corner. This floor is clear."

Sparrow sprinted, feet padding on the slick tile. She slowed as she rounded the corner to the main hallway.

One metallic door reflected the row of green lights lining the hallway.

"I see it," Sparrow said.

"Run through it," Rox replied.

"What?"

"Through it. Straight into the door."

"Rox..."

As Sparrow pleaded with Rox's disembodied voice, the door from the stairwell slid open. Sparrow didn't hesitate. She sprinted down the runway, like a plane preparing for flight. She could see numbered lights above the elevator as she grew nearer.

Seven.

Eight.

"Is that elevator for me?" Sparrow asked, still sprinting.

"What?" Rox replied, clearly caught off-guard. "No. No. No. Hurry, Sparrow. Run through it before it opens."

Nine.

Ten.

Sparrow put all her momentum forward. The door was coming into full view. The guards' voices were dull whispers behind her.

Eleven.

Twelve.

With eyes closed, she plowed headfirst into the metal door just as the digital ding sounded above her. A cold wind washed through her hair. Her feet still ran, but the ground was gone from beneath them. Sparrow opened her eyes and screamed.

She was outside of Ravenden.

Thirteen stories in the air.

"Rox!" she screamed as she closed her eyes again, the adrenaline still filling her veins.

"You did it!" Rox's voice sounded as if it came from on high.

"Help me, Rox, help!"

"Open your eyes," Rox said with a laugh. Sparrow lifted one eyelid. She was stuck in mid-air. "No time to enjoy the view. I think one of the guards saw you. They're investigating the door now. Hold on."

Sparrow now had both eyes open, and was taking it all in. Suddenly, she was jerked from her spot in the air, turned upside down, and descended head-first toward the ground. Her teeth clenched as she plummeted through the air. The ground grew closer and closer. Suddenly, she changed course and flew into the building.

She passed through the exterior metal wall, through dark, empty rooms, through windows, until she came to a familiar hallway. She was turned upright and landed on her feet in front of a large door.

"Huh?" A deep voice spoke behind her. The door slid open, and she stepped into the room. The door closed behind her, but a large security guard walked toward the window and looked inside.

"There's security all around this office. Couldn't bring you through the walls. Was able to hack the door, but..."

"Rox?"

Just then, the green lights lining the hallway turned

red. The security guard's watch flashed red. And the sound of a ship's horn filled the facility.

"Send the message—" Rox's voice cut out. Sparrow remembered Rox's instructions from the plan made back in Hoffgrid. It was only a matter of time until Rox was booted from the Ravenden server. Now, it was Sparrow's turn.

She ran toward Sulla's computer. Despite the chaos of the sirens and red flashing lights surrounding her, she breathed a sigh of relief when she was able to easily access Sulla's computer. Rox must have had time to disable the security protocols before she was kicked out.

Sparrow sat down and began the encrypted message sequence Rox had made her memorize. The lack of familiarity lead to errors, which lead to precious time wasted making sure the message was correct. She lost herself in the crude coding involved but was jolted from her trance when movement filled the windows before her.

Through the windows she saw the large room, Sanctuary One, stretching out into the distance. But, blocking her view from Sulla's crow's nest was a battalion of guards, rising to fill the glass windows, like they all stood on an invisible elevator. They wore black helmets that obscured their faces. Black, baggy military fatigues hid the bulk of their bodies. They hung in the air, like wasps ready to strike.

Sparrow focused all her attention back to the computer and began encoding the message with more speed and dexterity. An electric beep sounded behind her as the keypad chimed on the other side of the doorway.

She frantically searched the computer for the recipient of her message. She didn't need to turn around to know it was Sulla.

Just as the beeping stopped, Sparrow found what she was looking for. The door behind her slid open as she typed out the message.

"That's enough," the voice behind her said in a stern, calm voice, nearly drowned out by the alarm.

Just as she hit send, strong hands grabbed her arms and yanked her from the chair.

The giant hands threw Sparrow into the air, where she stuck like a fly on a trap. She couldn't move any part of her body, from her mouth to her big toe. She couldn't even blink, though she felt no desire to. Sulla walked beneath her niece, toward the only terminal in the room. The guards remained outside of the glass, forming a perimeter. Sulla's security guard stood by the open door.

"Locking me out of my own office. Not good." Sulla said. "What did that message say?" Sparrow felt her jaw loosen. She moved it around before replying.

"I ordered a pizza for us," Sparrow replied.

"What did it say?" Sulla repeated, louder this time.

"I just told you." Sparrow grinned.

"Bring in the other one," Sulla said, turning her attention to the hall. She made a gesture with her hand and Rox floated into the room, upside-down, like a discarded marionette. "You seem to be the smarter one," Sulla said, turning her attention to Rox. "Tell me, what's your game?"

"To get out of your stupid, sadistic simulation," Rox said before spitting toward Sulla.

"You two sure have some terrible language. Apparently, the Flaggers left their mark on you." She turned back to the terminal. Sparrow tried to make eye contact with her cousin, her co-conspirator, but she was frozen again. Sulla sat in the chair before the terminal but spun around to face the floating prisoners.

"How could someone do this?" Sulla said. "I know that's what you're thinking."

Sparrow remained motionless.

Sulla laughed. "No, no. I can't read your mind. Not yet anyway. We're working on it." She smiled. "How could someone lie about all of this, and kidnap their own family? I get it. It's complicated. You two brats have never had to compete with an older sibling.

"Your mommies grabbed the world by the cerebrum, and you could pick and choose whatever you wanted. Your mothers were virtual reality royalty, and you were the heirs toted around in expensive cars. The princesses of the virtual world."

Sparrow heard waves crashing in the distance.

"Do you know who invented the immersion tanks? The first immersion tank?" Sparrow felt her lips loosen, but she dared not speak. "No, you don't. No one cares about the actual technology. The hardware, the screws. Just hook me up and fly me to the moon." Sulla stood and walked toward Sparrow. She lowered her niece and looked her right in the eyes.

"It was me," Sulla said, inches from Sparrow's face. "Every tank in existence...my design. But what recognition does Sulla get? Nothing. FerVR steals my copyright, slaps their ghastly logo on it, and bullies me in court. So, how could someone do this? Build Ravenden? Build this simulation? It's the only logical conclusion in my mind.

"I was forced to build it. And I can't have you two spoiling my little secret. So, I'm going to ask you again, what did that message say?"

Sulla's eyes burned into Sparrow with an intensity Sparrow had seen only in her mother. She opened her mouth to speak but couldn't. Water filled her mouth, and there was no spitting it out or swallowing it down. She choked on the bitter liquid. Sulla's brows came together as confusion washed over her. Her aunt's confused face was the last thing she saw before the power went out.

TWENTY-ONE

Water filled the space around Sparrow's body. She felt goggles tight around her eyes. Only her face was out of the water. A thud knocked on the roof of the darkness. She screamed and pushed up on the solid darkness. A blinding light broke in like the first morning light.

Sulla was gone.

Sparrow lifted the lid of the tank until it stayed in the open position. She crawled out of the salt-water, wires snapping as she completed her demersion. She fell to her hands and knees beside the tank, water pooling on the rough concrete.

"Good show!" an unnatural voice echoed above her. She scrambled away from the sound. "My apologies. I certainly didn't mean to frighten you."

A small, matte black ball hung in the air above her. A green bank of lights shown around its equatorial line.

"Watzon!" Sparrow yelled. She stood and approached the bot.

"Yes, that is how I am commonly referred," it said with a slightly irritated tone. "Obviously, I received your message."

"We've got to find Mom and Rox and get out of here," Sparrow replied.

"Yes," Watzon replied. "The Roark is looking at us now."

Sparrow looked up to the office above her. The layout of the real Ravenden was the same as in the simulation, however, in the simulation, the near-dilapidated infrastructure of the physical Ravenden had been repaired virtually. Sparrow stood on the main floor, with hundreds of tanks before her. Sulla stood looking down at her through grimy windows.

Sparrow turned to one of the closed tanks and flipped open the lid. An elderly man startled awake. Sparrow went to the next one and found a young girl. She repeated this on all the tanks in her immediate vicinity, but with no luck.

"It appears three security guards will be here in twenty-seven seconds," Watzon said.

"Which way?" Sparrow asked.

Watzon flew off down a row of tanks in the opposite direction of Sulla's office. Sparrow followed, leaving the people behind her soaking wet and feeling the effects of demersion sickness. At the end of the current row, Sparrow could see an open doorway growing closer with every step.

As they got to the last row of tanks, Sparrow stopped. "This would make a great bo staff," she thought to herself as she kicked at the long metal bar that served as the handle to the tank. It began to loosen but wouldn't break off. Watzon flew back to her, extended a small, spider-like arm, and shot a thin beam of light on one end of the pole, then the other. The metal pole crashed to the ground like a cymbal.

"Thanks," Sparrow said as she lifted it. She maneuvered the metal bo staff like she had a thousand times during training, before gripping it firm, and following Watzon through the doorway.

"More stairs," Sparrow sighed.

"I'm sure those guards wouldn't mind carrying you," Watzon replied.

"Yeah, yeah," Sparrow said. "Can you find where they're keeping my mother?"

"One moment," Watzon said as the green light pulsed. "It was quite easy to infiltrate their server once you sent me that message. They really need better security. Found her."

"Where?"

"Trudy Hoodia and Teka Passer are being held in immersion tanks in the Roark's office."

"Of course, they are," Sparrow replied. "There will be guards everywhere."

"There appears to be a slight weak spot in the ceiling of her office," Watzon replied. A blueprint of the Ravenden infrastructure illuminated the space in front of them as they climbed the stairs. "If we reach the fifth floor, directly above her office, I believe I could cut a hole big enough for you to pass through."

"To the fifth floor," Sparrow replied. Despite the hurry, Sparrow's short legs confined her to taking the stairs one at a time. At every landing, she feared guards would spill from the doorway and grab hold of her. But, as she passed each number, metal bo staff in hand, the doors stayed closed.

They reached the fifth floor, and Watzon scanned for heat signatures in the hallway behind the door but found none. Still, Sparrow opened the door with caution and closed it with equal care.

"Following you," Sparrow replied. Watzon flew off down the hallway, Sparrow running behind, struggling to keep up. As Sparrow followed her robot friend over mangy carpet, with a bo staff in hand, a familiar feeling came over her. It was the peace of simpler days, before the Flaggers or The Stream or Ravenden. Before she could fully grasp the feeling, a familiar voice filled the hallway.

"You think you can hide, in my own building?" Sulla's voice echoed off the walls, coming from hidden speakers. "My guards are filling every stairwell, every floor, every room. Make this easy. Turn yourselves in."

Watzon hovered in front of a doorway. "We're here."

A door flew open in the distance, and a stampede of guards flooded through. Sparrow pushed the door open in a fury, and snapped it shut behind them. They stood in darkness. Watzon flicked on a small flashlight.

"Hurry, Watzon," Sparrow said.

"I'm afraid it's too late for that," a deep voice filled the room.

Sparrow jumped and held her bo staff at the ready. She had let her mother slip away from her too many times. Watzon pointed the flashlight in the direction of the voice. Sulla's personal security guard, looking the same as she did in The Stream, sat in the corner. She stood and held a small, black cylinder in her hand as she walked toward Sparrow.

"Cutting a hole in the ceiling? Really? I thought you were much smarter than that. It's been so long since I've had a good spar. We practice in The Stream, of course. But I'm old school. I like to feel the metal in my hands." She snapped the cylinder toward the ground, and it extended into four sections. In a split-second, the security guard struck Sparrow on the side of the head, lacerating a crimson arc above her right ear. Sparrow touched the wound in a frenzy, and brought back her hand, covered in fresh blood.

Seeing the blood took her back to the sewers under Zero City. The slain body of the Flagger she killed lay limp in her consciousness. She began to weep.

"I thought you were tougher than that," the security guard said.

"I won't do it," Sparrow replied. She threw the metal bo staff to the floor at the security guard's feet. "I just want my mother. That's all I've ever wanted. I never wanted to go to the city. I never wanted to kill that Flagger. I never wanted to come here. And I don't want to hurt you. I don't want anything from anyone. I just want my mother."

The security guard stared at Sparrow in silence. A range of emotions flashed on her face, still lit by Watzon's light. The stampede had caught up to them and was on the other side of the door, pawing at the lock. The security guard stomped toward Sparrow.

Sparrow closed her eyes.

The door opened.

"There's no one in here," the security guard said from the darkness. "Move up to sixth floor."

"Yes, ma'am," a man replied. Once the stampede was gone, the security guard grabbed Sparrow's arm.

The large woman pulled the door open. Light flooded the room. Sparrow squinted.

Once her eyes adjusted, she saw the security guard standing in the hallway, looking at her with a stone-cold stare.

"I would suggest you follow orders," Watzon said at a low volume. Sparrow agreed.

She followed the security guard down the hallway toward the stairwell. "No elevator?" Sparrow asked.

"Broke ten years ago," she replied without looking back.

Sparrow's short legs walked double-step to keep up, but her mind raced with the looming, inevitable confrontation, now nearly a reality. "What will I say to convince my aunt to let them go?" she thought. The security guard opened the door and led the way down the stairs. "How will I convince her to not banish me to some remote server in The Stream for the rest of my life?"

They reached the fourth floor and entered a hallway that was a run-down version of the hallway outside of Sulla's office she first encountered after waking up in Ravenden. Everything was faded and full of chips and cracks, but the door to the Roark' office remained unchanged. Sparrow squeezed her hand into a fist as they approached. Part of her regretted leaving the metal bo staff in the dark room, though, she knew she wouldn't have used it anyway. The security guard reached for the metal handle. Sparrow steeled herself for whatever would happen next.

The large woman pushed the door open, and Sparrow shuffled inside. Watzon flew over her shoulder. Only natural light filled the room. The glass windows lining the exterior had a thin layer of grime but remained pristine, otherwise. Sparrow could see the big room below with the tanks she had opened. The light flooded in from the row of windows along the ceiling of the main room.

The hum of machinery reverberated off the walls. Five tanks lay nestled on the left side of the room. The tiles beneath the tanks were cracked or missing completely. The tank farthest away was propped open. A beam of sunlight reflected off a puddle on the floor. A single chair sat near the windows opposite of the door they had just entered, looking out over the kingdom. It swayed back and forth.

Back and forth.

Slower and slower.

Until it stopped.

"The robot," a coarse voice said. She laughed a slow, sad laugh. "Bring it to me."

The security guard hesitated. She did not spare a glance at Sparrow before snatching Watzon out of the air. She delivered the metal sphere to her languid leader. Sulla turned the ball in her hand, cradling it like a newborn kitten.

"Where did you get this?" she asked.

"From your sister," Sparrow replied.

"Your mother?"

"No, Teka. Aunt Teka, at her estate."

"Teka?" Sulla replied. "She kept it?" The question turned into statement of realization. "She kept it."

Sparrow eyed the tanks, wondering which one her mother lay entombed in. She doubted the security guard would continue protecting her in the presence of Sulla, though Sparrow knew she might be stronger than the two of them, with their atrophied bodies from living in The Stream so long. But there was no desire for violence in her. No spark of raging fire anywhere in her bones. There was only one way she wanted to leave here...with her mother.

"Aunt Sulla," Sparrow said. "I'd like to go home now. With my mother."

"She finally got it to work," Sulla replied, still looking at Watzon.

"What?" Sparrow asked.

"This robot was mine," Sulla replied, looking up at Sparrow. "From a long time ago."

"It doesn't look that old," Sparrow replied.

"That's because I took great care of it. Updating more than the software. Hardware updates. A new motherboard. Upgraded optical sensor. Titanium propellor blades. I loved this bot."

"How did Teka get it?"

"She must have taken it when she moved out to her compound," Sulla said, still holding Watzon. "The old ice block does have a heart."

"That explains why it's so much different than Hobbes," Sparrow said to herself.

"Who's Hobbes?"

"My unit, like Watzon, but much older. It was a closed connection bot, of course."

"Was?" Sulla asked.

"We ran into some Flaggers in Zero City. Hobbes made a distraction for us. Mydoom pulled out a gun, and..." Sparrow couldn't finish. Her eyes flooded with tears, with a lump in her throat.

"Damn, Mydoom," Sulla replied. "Gave that man so many chances, but some code doesn't want to be refactored."

Sparrow didn't reply.

"So, my sister gave you my old bot as penance," she laughed to herself. "Sounds about right. Giving gifts that don't cost her. Bet you got a good shock at all the extra capabilities Watzon has."

Sparrow nodded. "I'd never seen so many mods on any piece of tech. I wish I could've known what they all did."

"What do you mean?"

"When Aunt Teka gave me Watzon, there were so many extra attachments and mods that it wouldn't even power on. Aunt Teka said she'd never been able to get it to work."

"That's because I added those so only someone who spent time with Watzon would be able to figure out..."

"That the output voltage was greater than the battery could supply," Sparrow interrupted. "It took me a few days to figure that out. I had plenty of time. It was a long walk."

Sulla's eyes flickered with life. Sparrow couldn't help but flash an innocent smile.

"You figured it out?" Sulla said as the realization washed over her. "But you live in the woods." A belly laugh erupted from Sulla. She laughed and laughed as she stood and walked toward Sparrow. "You used my own bot against me. Well done. Well done."

Sparrow took a step back.

"You have nothing to fear, child," Sulla said, walking toward the tanks. She had hoisted Watzon back into the air. "I never got to know my sisters. I was six when they left home. We became a family of micro-relations. Christmas and birthdays. I think Trudy came back for my graduation. I never wanted to be an only child."

Sparrow found herself nodding.

"You know better than most," Sulla said. "It's not that they didn't care, of course, they did. They said they did. They showed it. They got me stuff. I would have traded it all just to have them home to ride bikes around the neighborhood or to watch the immersion films until the sun came up. Watzon was the closest thing I had, and I would have given it up if it meant the room next to mine was occupied."

Sulla's words resonated deep into the well of Sparrow's own longing. In the weeks her mother was gone, the fire tower had been missing the spirit only the living can bring. She hated the feeling of being alone.

She knew she could become this woman, which she detested. Her jaw loosened and her shoulders rolled back. She uttered a phrase she never thought she would.

"You should come live with us," Sparrow said.

Sulla's gaze focused on her niece. Bewilderment and astonishment flashed across her face as micro-expressions. She opened her mouth a few times before remembering how to speak.

"Me? You'd have me live with you, after what I did?"

Sparrow nodded through tears.

"I don't understand you nature people," Sulla laughed. Sparrow smiled. "Now," Sulla continued, "let's get these tanks open.

TWENTY-TWO

Sulla walked slowly between two tanks and began pushing a sequence of buttons on the wall beside them. Sparrow moved to help her aunt, but the security guard rested her hand on Sparrow's shoulder. This grip was loose, but Sparrow understood.

She watched as her aunt fumbled around the rusting tank, gripping the bar with both hands, and pulling it open. She did the same thing to the middle tank. Now, three tanks lay with their lids open, and two remained sealed. Sulla went back to her seat and collapsed.

"Are you okay?" Sparrow asked her aunt.

"Yes, yes, just haven't been out here in a while," Sulla replied. She turned to the security guard. "See if we have any water. Drinkable water, will you?" The security guard nodded and left the room.

The sound of splashing erupted from the newly opened tanks. Sparrow's mother sat up first, pulling off the mask with violent rage. She crawled out of the tank and fell to the floor. Next, Teka sat up and pulled the mask from her face with methodical precision.

"Sparrow, run. Run!" her mother yelled after wiping her eyes and surveying the room.

"Mom, it's—"

"Go!"

"Always with the theatrics," Sulla said from her chair.

"Me? You kidnapped us!" Trudy yelled. She used the tank to pull herself up. "Let's go, Sparrow."

"Mom, wait," Sparrow replied. "She's not going to hurt us."

Trudy looked back to her younger sister sitting in the ripped, dusty chair. She looked around the room and found it in the similar dilapidated condition. Teka had also pulled herself out of the tank and was calibrating her vertical balance.

"What's going on here?" Teka said, speaking up for the first time and taking the words out of Trudy's mouth.

"Probably better coming from you," Sulla said, looking at Sparrow.

"Oh," Sparrow replied. "Remember the tour of Ravenden, the dinner, and all of that?"

"Earlier today?" Trudy replied, annoyed.

"Well, we've been in The Stream the whole time."

Trudy and Teka both snapped their heads toward their younger sister.

"Not bad, right?" Sulla replied.

"You did it," Teka replied, eyes now drifting out of focus. "You replaced reality, and..."

"It worked," Trudy butted in.

Sulla nodded.

"She's not going to hurt us," Sparrow replied.

"Hurt us?" Trudy replied. "Of course, she's not going to hurt us."

"Wait," Sparrow replied. "I thought you couldn't get hurt in The Stream. But my hand was still killing me from the bear attack."

"Bear attack?" Trudy said.

"You can feel pain, but you can choose to not get hurt," Sulla replied. "Those are two different things. You were already injured when you got here, so we had to make it feel real."

"Oh," Sparrow replied, looking at her bandaged hand.

"I think I've hurt you all enough," Sulla said as she turned her head away. "You can go, now."

Trudy opened her mouth, but no words came out. She started and stopped over the course of a few awkward seconds.

Finally, she turned to Sparrow. "Let's go home."

"Mom," Sparrow replied. She gave a slight head tilt to Sulla. Her mother closed her eyes, took a deep breath, then spoke the words she was trying to find just a moment ago.

"Sulla, come live with us," Trudy said.

Teka and Sulla turned their gaze toward their oldest sister in unison. Teka's brow furled. Sulla smiled and then laughed.

"You've raised an incredible daughter," Sulla replied.

"What do you mean?"

"She made me the same offer."

"There's another tower not too far away," Sparrow

replied. "You could live there. And Rox's house isn't too far away either. I think we'd all be in reach of the radio."

The three sisters laughed. Sulla walked over to her niece.

"Thank you, Sparrow." She extended her hand. Sparrow pulled her aunt into a hug. "But I still have to run this place. For now."

"Will you come visit, at least?"

"I've got to come by every now and then to make sure you're taking care of my bot, and to show you all the upgraded features."

Sparrow's eyes lit up like Watzon's flashlight module.

"You mean—"

"That's right. Take care of old Watzon for me."

"Thank you, Aunt Sulla!" Sparrow replied, pulling her aunt into another hug.

"Teka, you can travel back with us," Trudy said. "We'll make sure you get home safe."

"That's a laugh," Teka replied. "I don't think you're the one to give traveling advice. Now, if Sparrow's going, then I feel safe." They all laughed.

Sparrow's laugh faded first. "Aunt Sulla? There's one more thing."

"Your friend, Trax?"

Sparrow nodded.

"He wasn't doing well, as you know. My guards shot you all with the sleeping agent, and by the time they transported you back here, he didn't wake up." She paused and wiped her face. "I'm so sorry, Sparrow. I didn't mean to hurt anyone."

Sparrow felt a deep pressure in her head. She began to cry. She felt her mother's hand resting on her shoulder.

"Will you tell his family?" Sparrow whispered.

"They have been informed."

"Will they bury him?"

"They haven't replied."

A heavy, reverent silence filled the room. Only the sound of water droplets falling to the floor from the open tanks echoed off the walls. That sound gave Sparrow an idea.

"I'd like to take his body. He had one wish. Could you prepare it for me?" Sparrow asked.

"Of course," Sulla replied. "We'll start preparing it now. And we'll get you some supplies for your return trip. Let's go get cleaned up."

"And find Rox and Palo?" Teka added.

"Yes," Sulla replied.

"No tricks?" Trudy added.

"No tricks," Sulla replied.

"IF YOU HIT this nerve right here, it'll make them drop anything they're holding," Sparrow said, pointing to the ulnar nerve at the elbow. Snow was dripping off the limbs of the surrounding trees. The sun pierced through the canopy in light spears all around them. They walked in a slow-revolving circle as they continued their survival training. Watzon hovered over Sparrow's shoulder.

"What if it's a bear?" Rox asked.

"Run," Sparrow said.

Watzon's speakers roared to life with the deep growl

of a grizzly. Sparrow charged at Rox, but Rox had already turned and ran deep into the forest.

Sparrow hurdled large stones and fallen tree limbs in pursuit of her cousin but couldn't catch up. Rox had grown nimble and quick since moving to the castle with Sparrow and Trudy.

Sparrow lowered her head and ran in the highest gear she had but didn't gain any ground on her cousin. She ran past a small clearing where two large, jagged rocks had been used as headstones. Sparrow couldn't stop and pay her respects this time.

Rox darted between the trees a good thirty yards ahead. A wall of light lay ahead, and Sparrow knew they were coming to a clearing.

She could make up the gap in the open field. But, as Sparrow emerged from the line of trees, she realized she was at the foot of the castle. Rox was smiling from behind the locked fence surrounding the stairwell that led to their home.

"How was that?" Rox asked. Sparrow tried to pull the gate open, but it was stuck. "No way I'm letting a bear in here," Rox said.

They both laughed. Sparrow told Watzon to end the bear noises. Rox unlocked the gate.

"You passed," Sparrow said. "I think you're officially an 'outsider' now. How does it feel?" They began their ascent to the house. Rox was trying to find the right word. Halfway up the stairs, Rox replied.

"Right."

She looked around at the rolling treetops and the

snowcapped mountains and the shimmer off the lake. "It feels right. Thank you, Sparrow."

"Wouldn't be here without you,' Sparrow replied.

"Ahem," Watzon said with a robotic cough.

"Yeah, yeah," Sparrow replied with a smile. "We wouldn't be here without you either."

"This is one hundred percent true," Watzon replied.

"Kind of full of itself," Rox jabbed. "Like it contains access to the sum of human history or something."

"Have I mentioned my audio sensors are top of the line," Watzon replied.

They reached the top of the stairs and opened the door into the small living room. The girls were shocked to see three people standing around the stove.

"Mom?" Rox asked.

"Hello dear," Teka replied as dust swirled around inside of her body. "It's new hologram tech. Pretty neat, huh?"

"Yeah," Rox and Sparrow replied in unison.

"It was Sulla's idea," Trudy said. The floor creaked and the shadows shifted as she turned to face them. The third figure, ghost-like, spoke.

"I figure, if we can take physical people into a virtual world, we could also bring virtual people into the physical world," Sulla said.

"We think it might help people transition back to a physical existence, out of The Stream."

"Cool," Sparrow said.

"Bit of an understatement." Trudy laughed. "What are you girls up to?"

"I was going to give Rox another lesson on the new paramotor," Sparrow replied. "Over the lake this time."

"The lake?" Trudy asked.

"Yeah," Rox replied. "I think I'm ready."

"Very good," Trudy replied. "Teka?"

"Sounds good to me," the hologram replied. "Be safe girls."

"Yes, Mother," Rox replied.

"Well, then, back to it," Sulla replied. "Trudy, will you increase my opacity. I want to see how much power it consumes."

Trudy gave a sarcastic smile, waved to the girls, and returned to the hologram box on the counter. Sparrow and Rox, along with Watzon, climbed the stairs to their room.

After changing their clothes and preparing for their flight, Sparrow surveyed their bedroom. She spotted the small, corked bottle beside her bed, tucked it into her jacket pocket, and went down the ladder. When they closed the door to the castle, Trudy, Teka, and Sulla were talking back and forth at a breakneck pace.

Sparrow and Rox slid out the door without disturbing them. Circling the deck, they gathered up the new paramotor equipment and hauled it down the stairs and into the field below.

"Shall we run through the pre-flight checklist, Miss Sparrow?" Watzon said.

"Of course, we shall," Sparrow replied. "Rox, you're up."

"Got it," Rox said, squaring her shoulders back. "Parachute is first, right?"

"Correct," Sparrow replied. "Unfold the parachute and spread it out evenly along the ground, with the straps facing the direction of takeoff."

Once everything had been laid out, Sparrow pulled the propeller onto her back. Rox strapped into the harness in front of her. As Watzon hovered in front of Rox, she snatched their robot friend out of the air and clipped it onto her vest. Sparrow pulled the parachute into the air. The two conjoined cousins hobbled around as air filled the parachute.

"Run!" Sparrow yelled. They bounced down the path, like the first moon landers as the wind caught their sail. Their feet no longer touched the ground.

Rox pushed the button in her hand, causing the propeller to whirl to life. As Sparrow held the strings in both hands, she pulled down with her right hand, causing them to bank around the castle and head toward Reelfoot Lake.

Once they reached a comfortable altitude, Rox cut the engine.

"Good work," Sparrow said above the wind.

"Best takeoff yet," Rox replied. "Are you ready?"

Sparrow put her hand to the bottle in her pocket and replied, "Yes."

The sunlight split the still surface of the lake. If Sparrow didn't know better, she would have thought they were looking down upon a giant mirror. But the fact was, she did know better. She had done this many times, more than she could remember. But she wouldn't forget this time.

"I'm going to take us down slow," Sparrow said. Rox

gave a thumbs up and they started their descent. It didn't take long to get below the tree line. Sparrow handed the controls to Rox, who held them steady, circling just above the lake. Sparrow pulled the bottle from her pocket.

"This is Reelfoot Lake," Sparrow said. A tear rolled off her cheek into the lake. "I hope you like it here, friend." She pulled the cork from the bottle, took a deep breath, and turned it over. Grey ash drifted out and found its forever home lounging on the warm surface of the lake.

ABOUT THE AUTHOR

F.C. Shultz is an author and poet whose work has been published in Ekstasis Magazine, Every Day Fiction, and the *Of Gods and Globes* anthologies. He's published a handful of middle grade and young adult novels.

He's trying to cultivate a deep appreciation for the simple pleasures, which means writing a lot of poems about birds (and novels about dragons). He lives in the Midwest with his wife and two kids.

You can find stories and other author resources at fcshultz.com.

ABOUT THE PUBLISHER

Daath Stone Books exists to publish fantastical kidlit for fantastic kids. We don't write down for children. In fact, we do the opposite. We believe our best work should be for children.

Find more fantastical books at **daathstonebooks.com.**

www.ingramcontent.com/pod-product-compliance
Lightning Source LLC
LaVergne TN
LVHW091249110826
845146LV00002BA/711

* 9 7 9 8 9 9 3 0 3 0 7 2 2 *